2.00

BELLRINGER STREET

Also by Robert Richardson:
The Latimer Mercy

BELLRINGER STREET

Robert Richardson

St. Martin's Press
New York

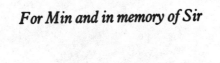

For Min and in memory of Sir

Author's note

Those who know – and particularly those who live in – Fore Street and the neighbourhood of Old Hatfield, Hertfordshire, should be assured that only some local architecture and geography have been borrowed. All the events of this book are invented and the various characters who experience them are of imagination all compact.

BELLRINGER STREET

Chapter One

Breaking off from idly pecking at the ground, an iridescent, bejewelled peacock raised its head and surveyed Augustus Maltravers with disdain, before turning its back and walking dismissively away with the *hauteur* of a Duke who has been approached by some upstart to whom he had not been introduced. Watching the bird's slightly tatty Argusian tail sweep the ground like a train in its wake, Maltravers felt that such behaviour embodied attitudes no longer appropriate as noble and time-hallowed families clung doggedly to their Stately Homes of England. Peacocks were now kept as an additional attraction for paying visitors, not as ornamental and suitably toffee-nosed pets of the wealthy, titled and privileged in their private gardens. He looked beyond the bird at a further manifestation of such diminished glories; the impressive seventeenth-century pile of Edenbridge House, formidable focus of the twelve hundred acres of Edenbridge Park, principally farmed but still patched with residual rustic woodlands and open fields.

"One day, my boy," he promised, "all this will be somebody else's."

Ten-year-old Timothy Penrose was unimpressed.

"Please can we have an ice lolly?" he asked, generously including his younger sister Emma in the request.

"A modest enough demand. Here you are."

Maltravers produced coins from his pocket and the children raced off towards a nearby ice-cream van, their enthusiasm for Martian Monsters of singularly sickly flavour vastly exceeding impossible dreams of very upmarket real estate ownership. Left with Tess Davy, the established natural lady in his life, Maltravers returned his attention to the home of the Earls of Pembury.

"Now that's just the sort of little place in the country I'd like, please," Tess told him as they admired its domed square towers and redbrick Gothic chimneys thrusting upwards above regular grids of windows with diamond-patterned lead lighting, each crowned with a classical ornamental moulding. "I was made for the lifestyle."

She whirled round and the professional actress in her conjured up the instant impression that pencil-thin jeans and floppy T-shirt had been transmuted into a less practical but greatly more elegant crinoline. Her startling green eyes shimmered impishly before her pre-Raphaelite cascade of russet hair and Gainsborough face dipped in mock obeisance.

"Welcome to our simple home, my Lord." The trace of huskiness in her everyday voice had disappeared, replaced by slightly over-genteel cadences belonging to another woman held in the graceful half-curtsey. Certain attitudes, however, remained intact. "My parents are away but they bade me make you welcome – my room's the fourth along on the first floor." She raised her lowered head and looked at him again, a face of virtuous innocence framing eyes glittering with knowing carnality.

"I may stay for some time," Maltravers replied. "I think I'm going to like this place."

"You'd better believe it," Tess told him tersely, the invisible crinoline cast off as swiftly as it had been created as she straightened up and looked back at the house. "How much do you think it would cost?"

"More than any writer of my level of success will ever make," Maltravers told her. "Jeffrey Archer could just about afford the down payment on the outhouse, assuming they have such a thing. The Earl of Pembury would make the average millionaire look comparatively penniless."

Maltravers was right to a degree, in that the recently elevated twelfth Earl did not lie awake at night worrying about the odd hundred thousand pounds here or there, but the sublimely balanced architectural geometry and discreet grandeur of Edenbridge House disguised the fact that it had been undergoing a financial earth tremor as rising taxes and other troublesome fiscal legislation threatened it sorely. The roots of the problem had been planted by the eleventh Earl, who had survived for a formidable ninety-seven years, stubbornly insisting on passing the last of them in the same secure and pleasant manner as he had enjoyed the first. Subtle accountants had repeatedly tried to persuade him of the advantages offered by the law in the form of tax havens, allowable expenses and other cunning loopholes, but he had loftily dismissed them from his presence and only agreed to open his home to the paying public when forced to do so by unforgiving necessity. He had surveyed the invasion of the masses with distaste, before grumpily retiring to the West wing with his memories to devote his remaining years to the completion of his autobiography *From Enfant Terrible to Éminence Grise*; in a somewhat pedestrian life, he had failed to fulfil either role, but the title had come to him one day and he adamantly refused to abandon it. Increasingly reclusive and resentful, he had resolutely regarded the Chancellor of the Exchequer and all his works as not worthy of the attention of an English gentleman, and Edenbridge's cash crisis had grown with his years. When death had abruptly turned off the old man's heart while he was shaving one morning, his son felt sorrow but also considerable relief that some very pressing matters could finally be given overdue attention. A brief reading of the uncompleted life story offered little prospect of profitable publication and it was despatched to the less accessible regions of the Edenbridge archives. Having placed his father (fully shaved) in the family vault with proper ceremony, the new Lord Pembury had speedily called back the accountants to put his ancient house in order.

Thus, while in the guidebooks Edenbridge House remained a great stately home, saturated with treasure and heavy with history, it was now in effect the head office of a limited company with Lord Pembury occupied with much the same sort of business decisions as the managing director of a boot factory. The previously token gift shop in the old kitchens had been massively enlarged, selling everything from elegant cut glass to tacky kitsch plastic place mats (tourists' tastes covered a range as wide as their means and all had to be catered for) and plans were in hand to establish a safari park in the grounds. Meanwhile, death duties, the inescapable companions of the event itself, were still metaphorically standing at the gate, sternly demanding satisfaction in connection with the latest reduction in the family numbers. Negotiations concerning the State's acceptance of the great Rubens at the turn of the stairs were at an advanced stage, with the Canaletto in the library under consideration to make up the balance. The Pemburys, who had dined for a hundred years ignoring the growing spectre of Socialism at the feast, were demonstrating great skill at learning the precautions required to hang on to the family silver.

The children returned, each happily clutching a repulsive icy amalgam of water and disgusting artificial flavouring in vivid maroon.

"There's a joke on the stick," Timmy announced delightedly, then sucked the obscene object with juvenile rapture, revealing that what taste he had did not extend to his mouth. Maltravers sighed; the general level of wit on lollipop sticks was dire and it seemed unjust that his generosity to his friends' children should result in him being subjected to it.

"Come on, let's get you home," he said. "We should arrive just in time for those things to have ruined your appetite for lunch."

They turned away from the house and made their way through the crowds of visitors wandering about the park and gardens. Serious and efficient Germans consulted their guidebooks and meticulously ticked off items of interest they had seen;

perpetually cheerful Japanese, festooned with cameras of incredible complexity though small size, looked endlessly polite over a heritage that was comparatively recent by their culture; well-padded and flamboyant Americans were vaguely overawed by so much antiquity but found the local variety of the hot dog criminally deficient; the English, who are generally appallingly ignorant about their history, were unmoved by such a richness of it. All of them looked overcooked in the burning midday sun that hammered down on the stable yard with its cafeteria and toilets, casting slate-edged shadows on brick walls like the lining of a furnace. Everybody moved slowly between the immense dark green yew bushes that lined the drive leading to the house and the roofs of the multicoloured patchwork of vehicles in the car park were crowned with a trembling film of heat.

"Are you going to the concert tonight?" Timmy asked as they passed through the dark-shadowed, two-storey brick arch of the Bellringer Street lodge gate; a middle class upbringing had included proper instruction in the manners of polite conversation.

"Yes," said Tess. "Are you?"

"No way. It sounds awful," the boy replied, twisting his head at an unnatural angle to capture an escaping lump of rapidly melting ice. "I'm going to watch *Superman II* on the video again. It's dead good."

"There are those who think Old English music is dead good," Maltravers observed. "Although they usually express it rather more elegantly."

"It's boring," Timmy pronounced conclusively. "There's no beat."

"Well, it's not quite Duran Duran country," Maltravers admitted. "But it does have its points."

The boy regarded him with renewed and unexpected interest. On previous occasions when they had met, he had found the tall, loose-limbed man with the amused blue eyes in a face

II

drawn in long, vertical lines passable company for someone so old – Maltravers was thirty-five – but it had never occurred to him that he might have some familiarity with contemporary rock bands. Despite his serious reservations about someone who actually quoted poetry in everyday conversation, he was favourably impressed.

"Do you like them?" he asked.

"I prefer Tears for Fears, but Duran are very good," Maltravers told him. Timmy returned his attention to his lollipop, still unconvinced of the qualities of Old English music but becoming vaguely aware of the possibility that the company of some grown-ups might not actually be a total waste of time.

They passed through the huge wooden lodge gates and back into the blinding heat, with St Barbara's parish church on their left and the hundred yards of parallel terraced houses that made up Bellringer Street dropping steeply down the hill in front of them. The street was frequently loosely described as Georgian but in fact contained a range of styles from late Regency to post-Victorian. The bricked-in archway in the wall rising to their right had once been an entrance for stage coaches when the twenty miles or so from Capley to London had been a day's journey and the building, now converted into flats, was one of eight hostelries which the street had contained to cater for their passengers. Now only the ghosts of the pubs remained, immortalised in a verse written by one of their long-dead customers –

> Candlestick, Kingmaker,
> Arms of the baker,
> Sun in the morning
> And parson's retreat.
> Cricketer, virgin
> And coach driver urging,
> These are the taverns of Bellringer Street.

Maltravers found it an agreeable thought that at one time a pint in every one – Candlestick, Earl of Warwick, Baker's Arms, Rising Sun, Pulpit, Batsman, Maid's Head and Coach and Horses in inebriated descent down the hill – would have resulted in a very pleasantly accumulated hangover. Lamentably, all were now converted into private houses with the exception of the Batsman which remained about halfway down to pursue its decent calling and – thanks be to God – the noble efforts of those dedicated to the preservation of real ale ensured that it still served beer infinitely more drinkable than the hideous chemical urine mass-produced in an evil flood by the giant brewery combines. The double-sided sign, suspended from the ancient, swirling iron bracket protruding at right angles above the pub door, portrayed the patriarchal image of W. G. Grace and, whether looking up or down the hill, the cricketing doctor surveyed the most expensive and select of residences. Bellringer Street was now a very good address in the estate agents' league table; its assorted collection of weathered bricks, imposing front doors, occasionally plastered façades, varied windows and rippled roofs of tiles or slate increasing in value almost between the rising and setting of each day's sun. Even the absence of front gardens, which meant stepping from each house on to paving slabs cracked, battered and patched like a crude jigsaw, was presented to potential purchasers as further evidence of a unique and enviable lifestyle.

For Bellringer Street was now in Old Capley, a name jealously guarded by its residents to disassociate themselves from the post-war Capley New Town which had been gracelessly stuck on to the western edges of the original. A distant prospect of its high-speed motorway, high-rise flats and high-intensity shopping centre was visible from the top of Bellringer Street, but ancient and modern maintained somewhat separate existences, each darkly suspecting the other of either well-heeled snobbishness or a deplorable habit of not bathing regularly. Both attitudes were seriously flawed, but class prejudice is a two-way street – or avenue.

With the commercial activity of the town moving westward with the new development, Old Capley had become something of a pleasant residential backwater, although a handful of local shops still survived in the square at the bottom of the hill, including a mail order establishment catering for those with a taste for erotic underwear and bedroom attire not conducive to a quiet night's sleep. This undertaking was regarded ambivalently. While it was clearly deplorable that persons of irregular sexual habits should apply to an address in Old Capley for their supplies of peep-hole bras or black suspender belts, the proprietor of the enterprise, a quietly-spoken, middle-aged man with teenage daughters of unquestioned purity, was both a sidesman at St Barbara's and a visible supporter of the Conservative Party. That both the Church of England and Tory Central Office might have numbered several of his customers among their members had occurred to Maltravers on previous visits, but he had prudently not voiced such an outrageous suggestion. For no particular reason, he was contemplating the intriguing possibility again as they walked away from the lodge gates and Timmy came up with an unexpected question.

"How do you stop a rhinoceros charging?" The Martian Monster had been devoured and the legend on its stick exposed.

"I have the dreadful feeling you're going to tell us," Maltravers replied.

"Take away his credit cards!" Timmy hooted with laughter, revealing an interesting familiarity with modern finance in one so young.

"Not bad by lollipop standards," Maltravers admitted. "Come on, Emma, let's get it over with. What does yours say?"

The little girl was examining her stick in some mystification. "I can't read it," she announced, and offered it to Maltravers who peered at it gravely.

"Help. My name is Lord Lucan and I am a prisoner in a lollipop factory," he said, straight-faced.

"Give it to me," said Tess. "Right. What goes quack and has water coming out of its head?"

"She said it, she actually said it," Maltravers muttered in disbelief.

"What?" demanded the children.

"Moby Duck."

"What might be called a children of Ishmael joke," Maltravers commented, and was contemplating the possible commercial rewards in a singularly odd field of creative writing as they entered what had once been the entrance to the public bar of the Warwick Arms, now the kitchen of Peter and Susan Penrose's home. Standing on the corner of a rough-stoned right of way opposite the church gates, it was a house curiously piled upwards from capacious cellar, through kitchen and dining room on the ground floor, sitting room and bedroom one floor up and the two remaining bedrooms upstairs again. As they walked in, Susan, a walking advertisement for motherhood and Laura Ashley, was producing some sort of lunchtime organisation out of comfortable chaos and Peter was engrossed in the Araucaria crossword in the *Guardian*.

"In game, I am gen," he announced runically, looking up at Maltravers. "Two words of six and ten letters, second word begins with a V."

"I noticed that before we went out." Maltravers looked at the puzzle over Peter's shoulder. "I have been giving it considerable thought during our walk and still haven't the remotest idea."

The two men had originally met while working together as reporters on the *Worcester Evening Echo*, sharing a passion for cricket, crosswords and similar indecent ambitions regarding the body of Susan in the accounts department. Observing where Susan's preferences lay, Maltravers had diplomatically withdrawn his attentions and had subsequently been best man at their wedding. Although their careers had drifted apart – Maltravers into enough success as a playwright to pay most of the bills and now a first novel and Peter into something mysterious with the BBC World Service – they saw each other regularly. The current visit followed Maltravers' completion of his book and also the end of the run of a play in which Tess had been appearing. Their plans for the week centred mainly on driving into the neighbouring countryside in search of historic buildings, preferably with attendant decent pubs, and Maltravers had also agreed to turn out for the Edenbridge Estate side in their annual cricket match against the Capley Town team. His appearance had been requested at the last minute following an incident involving an Estate player, stepladders and a greenhouse roof, which had resulted in the smell of broken glass and a liberal application of plaster to his person. It was some years since Maltravers had played, but he reasoned that the standards would not be such as to embarrass him.

They settled variously around the table, Maltravers regarding Susan's burstingly pregnant form with misgiving as she lowered herself into a chair. The arrival of the third Penrose seemed alarmingly imminent and his knowledge of what to do in such circumstances was as limited as his understanding of how his car worked; a microscopic advance from nil. Susan had earlier said that the event was still two weeks away but such a further period of abdominal inflation seemed inconceivable. Had his own dismantled marriage produced children, Maltravers would have been better informed but, as it was, close encounters with prodigious female ripeness caused him unease. He fervently hoped that the infant would at least have the decency to wait until they had finished eating.

With four – strictly speaking, four and a half – adults, two children, and a Golden Labrador puppy of excitable temperament occupying the kitchen, polite conversation became difficult and Maltravers joined Peter in further consideration of the uncompleted crossword.

"In game, I am gen," he repeated thoughtfully. "Some reference to game birds perhaps? Grouse has six letters if that's any help."

"Enigma Variations," Tess said from the other end of the table. "Pass the couscous please, darling."

Maltravers stared at her. "Pardon?"

"The couscous. It's right by you."

"No, not that. How did Elgar suddenly get in here?"

"It's the answer," Tess said simply. Both men regarded her blankly. "The answer to the clue . . . in the crossword."

"We know where the clue is," Maltravers said. "But we don't understand your reasoning."

"The words 'In game' and 'I am gen' are both anagrams of 'Enigma'," she explained patiently. "So they're both variations, aren't they? Now can I have the couscous please?"

Peter turned back to the crossword in surprise and filled in the solution as Maltravers passed the bowl across, looking wonderingly at Tess as though she had suddenly started speaking in fluent Greek.

"Madam, I have known you in all meanings of the word for a long time," he said. "Now I find you can solve crossword clues. You've never shown the slightest interest in them before."

"Of course not. I can never understand why you waste your time with them. Thank you." Tess accepted the bowl and put her tongue out at him.

"How do I love thee?" Maltravers asked. "Let me count the ways. You're marvellous in bed and now I find I can talk to you about crosswords afterwards. Children, you didn't hear that."

Difficult questions from Timmy or Emma about earthy interpretations of Elizabeth Barrett Browning were averted by the wall-mounted telephone ringing next to where Peter was sitting. Occupied with his meal and further wrestling with the labyrinthine workings of Araucaria's mind, Maltravers was only half aware of Peter's end of the conversation, although he gathered that some manner of unlikely news was being imparted. Peter's "You're joking!" followed by inquiries as to why and when something was to happen sounded vaguely interesting.

"Who was that?" Susan asked as he rang off.

"Frank Dunham. He says that Lady Pembury wants Tom Bostock buried – and would you believe in the family vault?"

"After all these years?" Susan was visibly amazed. "What on earth's come over her?"

"Conscience, it seems."

Maltravers rapidly considered this exchange and found it wanting. Bodies, in his experience, were generally buried or become part of the smoke nuisance over crematoria reasonably soon after decease; leaving them lying around was inconvenient, untidy and unhygienic. But it seemed that the body of Tom Bostock – whoever he was – had remained undealt with for a period measurable in years. Surely someone should have stepped in and attended to its disposal before the latest Lady Pembury made it her business? He remained silent, awaiting enlightenment.

"Well, the tourists won't like it," Susan added.

"Nothing's going to happen until after the house closes at the end of the season in October," Peter told her. "They'll reprint the guidebook for next year and there's no reason why they can't still sell the postcards, unless Lady Pembury thinks even that's out of order. Frankly, I'm not that surprised. Tom was a member of the family even if he was a bastard."

All in all, Maltravers found this raised more questions and afforded no answers. The references to Lady Pembury, tourists and guidebooks clearly appeared to locate matters in Edenbridge House – where they must also sell postcards – but none of this was helpful. And did Peter mean "bastard" in the literal or pejorative sense? Whichever the case, a final resting place among the great and the good of the Pemburys in their private chapel in St Barbara's seemed a curiously excessive gesture.

"Surely it won't be a proper funeral though?" Susan queried.

"Apparently that's what her Ladyship wants," Peter replied. "She feels that the family owes a duty to old Tom – she's concerned about his immortal soul. You know what she's like."

Susan's nod showed that she evidently did. "Well, it will be interesting to see how many mourners turn up . . . Gus, more of anything?"

"Nothing more to eat, but a little explanation would be welcome," said Maltravers. "You do realise your conversation has had a rather Pinteresque quality don't you? As I understand it, Lady Pembury wants to organise a funeral for someone who died some time ago. Right?"

"He was hanged in 1778," said Peter.

"That," Maltravers conceded, "is some time ago. What was the hold-up? Wouldn't the coroner release the body?"

"Haven't you ever seen Tom Bostock when you've been here before?" asked Susan.

"From what I've just heard, I'm sure I'd remember if I had," Maltravers said with conviction. "Meeting a 200-year-old corpse would tend to stick in the memory."

Peter leaned back in his chair and pulled open the drawer of the stripped pine Welsh dresser behind him. He rummaged about for a moment then produced a thin booklet, flicked through the pages and handed it open to Maltravers.

"Read that. It explains everything."

The booklet, called *Capley: No Ordinary Town*, was a potted history written by the editor of the local newspaper, and the page Peter offered Maltravers was part of the section on Edenbridge House and the Pemburys, illustrated with a picture of a full-size skeleton in an open coffin.

"Undoubtedly the most unusual feature of the house is the skeleton of Tom Bostock in the cellar," he read. "He was born about 1750, the illegitimate son of the third Earl and the daughter of one of his tenant farmers, from whom he appears to have inherited a rebellious nature. Incensed at being denied the privileges afforded his legitimate half-brother, later the fourth

Earl, he left Capley at about the age of fourteen to pursue a criminal life in London. He returned to the area some ten years later and became a notorious highwayman, terrorising the stagecoach traffic which then regularly passed through the town. There was little of the romance or glamour frequently associated with such activities about him and the fourth Earl, who had by then succeeded to the title, called him 'an abominable ruffian and disgrace to the family name'.

"Having escaped capture on a number of occasions, Bostock appears to have become remarkably foolhardy and was finally arrested in the Maid's Head public house in Bellringer Street in June, 1778, where he was in bed with his mistress. Trapped in the room by the authorities, he leapt from the window but injured himself in his fall.

"Tried and convicted at the Autumn Assizes, he was hanged in Capley Marketplace after which his body was placed in an iron cage by the side of the London road on the outskirts of the town as a warning to others. When only the skeleton remained, the fourth Earl claimed possession of it and, it was assumed at the time, had it buried. In fact he instructed that it be kept in the cellar of Edenbridge House and throughout his lifetime drank an annual toast over the coffin to the damnation of Tom Bostock's soul. After the fourth Earl's own death, the family were in some embarrassment as to what they should do with the remains and in fact did nothing. The skeleton remained in its coffin in the cellar for nearly two centuries.

"When Edenbridge House was opened to the public, it was decided to include the coffin and its contents as part of the guided tour. Despite the grisliness of the relic and the questionable conduct of the fourth Earl, Tom Bostock's skeleton has proved a popular attraction at Edenbridge and the coloured postcard of him (see illustration) has consistently been the best seller in the tourists' shop.

"It is a strange irony that Tom Bostock, denied any rights in

Edenbridge House in his lifetime, today enjoys more fame there than either his father or legitimate half-brother."

Maltravers finished reading and passed the booklet across the table to Tess.

"What can a mere writer of fiction do against a story like that?" he asked. "Oddly enough I've never been in the house – it's usually been closed for the winter when I've been before – so I've never seen him. However, I must make a point of doing so before he disappears. But why does Lady Pembury want him buried all of a sudden?"

"Lady Pembury comes from a family that always does the right thing," Peter explained. "Making money out of the dead they would consider tacky, and denying them a Christian burial is very bad form. She couldn't do anything while the old man was alive, but now she is mistress of Edenbridge House and can follow her conscience."

"But of course we will wait until after the current tourist season is over," Maltravers remarked somewhat cynically. "Business before conscience. However, it's all splendidly ridiculous and I may make a point of attending the . . . good Lord! It's another anagram."

His attention had switched back to the crossword in the paper, still lying folded on the table in front of him.

"Do you know that 'Contaminated' can be reshuffled into 'No admittance'? How very appropriate."

Maltravers had been about to say that he might attend Tom Bostock's funeral for the novelty value of the occasion. When he eventually did so some months later, he was to experience a sense of sorrow he could not have imagined that summer afternoon.

Chapter Two

The oboe poured a pure, plaintive top C through the Great Hall
of Edenbridge House. It held for seven and a half quavers then
the finespun thread of sound tumbled through B and A natural
and wandered down in the minor key until it reached the C an
octave below the first. The final two notes were repeated, then
the instrument glided into the flowing theme of *Greensleeves*,
the reedy, mellifluous notes placid as slow-moving water
beneath overhanging leaf-laden trees.

From his seat by one of the high windows, Maltravers gazed
out into the gleaming evening. The music evoked a romantic
legend of the past in which the manifest inconveniences –
indeed, the downright nastinesses – of Tudor life were replaced
by false but seductive images. A great Queen and her witty
court (all stinking to high heaven in truth) and a cheerful
population of country folk living contented merry lives and
drinking good ale (in fact, generally starving and dying from
revolting diseases) were conjured up by gentle melody. Maltravers was quite prepared to suspend knowledge of the reality
and bask in the deception as dwindling twilight seeped through
the graceful, oak-panelled, marble-floored hall with the six
musicians gathered in a pool of electric yellow at one end.

His pleasure was not shared by Lord Pembury, the possessor
of an unrivalled private collection of original New Orleans jazz
recordings, who found the proceedings tedious. He had only
agreed to the concert taking place in the interests of Edenbridge
Estates Ltd, with particular reference to the safari park scheme,
which called for a number of prerequisites of which land,

finance negotiated at suitable rates and appropriate lifestock were but three; there was also the question of planning permission from Capley District Council. While the park would be on Pembury's private property, he could not just replace the cows and fallow deer currently grazing there with much less docile beasts as it suited him. Ever mindful of the welfare of its ratepayers, the council would at least wish to ensure that security met required standards; people being chewed up by escaped lions was considered contrary to public health regulations. While totally above bribery and corruption – the family motto was "The sword never rusts" – the Earl had a prudent eye towards the right people. When the chairman of the council had tentatively suggested the use of Edenbridge House to stage a concert in aid of his appeal for a hospice for the dying, Lord Pembury had readily agreed. Looking after his father, whose pestiferous longevity had been painfully expensive, made him sympathetic to such an institution and he reasoned it could be advantageous to scratch the back of the town's first citizen in the hope that the members of the planning committee might collectively scratch his in return. The result was that the dulcet melodies of Tallis and his sixteenth-century contemporaries were now being heard within the same walls that had once throbbed to the cornet of Louis Armstrong leading his band as they pounded out "Mamma Don't Allow" during a private concert four hundred years later. Maltravers found the contrast exquisite.

The music faded into polite applause and well-bred murmurings of aesthetic appreciation (others had roared, stamped and leapt to their feet for Satchmo) and a man of alarming height, wearing a precariously balanced toupee as conspicuous as melted cheese poured over a cauliflower, stood up and began thanking everyone in sight. His chain of office identified him as the council chairman, a man who, Peter had told Maltravers earlier, had now abandoned his youthful Marxist convictions for secret hopes of at least an MBE. He earned several Brownie points with fulsome comments on the "great generosity of Lord and Lady Pembury" – a phrase Maltravers counted six times with slight variations – before Lady Pembury rewarded him with a somewhat strained smile and invited everyone through to the Long Gallery where wine and coffee were being served. Maltravers and the others joined the throng shuffling through corridors of understated, casual opulence.

"I say, this is rather splendid," Maltravers observed as they entered the gallery. Nearly one hundred and fifty feet from end to end with windows all down one side facing floor-to-ceiling bookcases on the other, it was broken in the centre by an immense fireplace crafted from enough marble to provide tombstones for most of the population of Old Capley and topped with a larger-than-life statue of Charles II. Fruit, flowers and heraldic devices swept among the swirling plaster-work of the ceiling and the floor was covered along its centre with what was claimed to be the largest Indian carpet in the world.

"Long enough to have a bowling alley in the back," Maltravers added approvingly. "I could get quite used to this sort of thing."

They collected their wine and went to look out of one of the windows from which they could see the long, double line of decorative chestnut trees marching down what had for centuries been the main entrance to Edenbridge House, now fallen into decayed disuse. What had formerly been the formidable approach to the might of the Pemburys, along which at least seven monarchs and their courtiers had travelled, looked neglected and strangely sad. Current plans had most of the area earmarked for a coach park.

"Good evening, Peter," a voice said behind them.

They turned towards a pale man of about thirty whose good looks would have been effeminate had it not been for an indisputably masculine construction of the jawline and an athletic leanness of body indicating muscular strength. Maltravers noticed the most fleeting expression of discomfort flicker across his face as his eyes caught Susan's and she rather obviously turned her back on him and looked out of the window again.

"Hello, Simon," said Peter. "I didn't realise you were here. This is Gus Maltravers and Tess Davy who are staying with us for a few days. Gus is filling in for Ian in the Town match tomorrow." He turned to Maltravers. "Lord Dunford, who will eventually inherit all this lot. But he answers to Simon."

The handshake Maltravers received from the slender fingers momentarily squeezed with crushing pressure and he frowned slightly as he looked at Dunford's albescent, symmetrical features.

"Simon," he repeated, as though trying to link some connection in his mind. "And the Pembury family name is Hawkhurst . . . and so you must be Simon Hawkhurst who got a cricket Blue at Oxford and played for Middlesex for a couple of seasons. Am I right?"

Dunford smiled. "I'm very flattered you remember. I didn't use the title in those days."

"Peter, if this is the standard of your Estate team, you might have let me know," Maltravers said reproachfully. "I'd have thought twice about appearing in such company. At one time they were talking about Simon as an England opener."

"A long time ago," Dunford corrected. "You've nothing to worry about. Most of the Estate side are like Peter here – all cross-bat swipes and beer guts."

He prodded Peter's stomach, which gave under his fingers like a beach ball.

"Susan, you're feeding him too well."

The innocuous remark carried the finest edge of forced cordiality, underlined by Dunford's uncertain glance at Susan's back as he made it. She did not turn round but her shoulders stiffened as she drew in her breath as though controlling herself. Her ill manners and Dunford's discomfort were becoming noticeably tangible.

"Anyway, I'm sure Alister and I can hold the rest of you together," Dunford added, hastily covering Susan's resonant silence. Tess looked from one to the other, picking up vibrations and trying to identify them.

"Who's Alister?" Maltravers asked as Tess raised one fine eyebrow at him quizzically.

"Alister York, my father's secretary," Dunford explained, turning to face him as though grateful for the opportunity to cover Susan's rudeness. "First-rate batsman. Played in the Minor Counties league a few years ago and . . ."

Only Peter seemed unaware of Susan's hostility as she suddenly turned round and interrupted.

"Simon, you do realise this is Tess Davy the actress, don't you?" The words were an introduction, the entire tone a curt reprimand. Maltravers reflected that it was certainly not the way in which a member of the English aristocracy was accustomed to being spoken to in his own home – or anywhere else for that matter. The remarkable thing was that, far from being offended, Dunford was instantly apologetic.

"No, I . . . I'm dreadfully sorry, Miss Davy. I should have recognised you at once. How unforgivable."

Tess had the immediate impression that Dunford was not apologising to her. For a moment he was not even speaking to her, but looked straight at Susan as though seeking some sort of forgiveness.

"I saw you as Judith Paris on television last year," Dunford added, turning his attention from Susan, giving the suggestion of being relieved that she had at least acknowledged his presence. "You were marvellous. You made me read all the *Herries Chronicles* again."

"Thank you," Tess said, then glanced at Susan, waiting to see what she would say next. She said nothing but lowered her face towards the glass in her hands and Tess was standing close enough to see that she was biting her lip.

"Are you . . . er . . . appearing in anything at the moment?"

Maltravers appreciated Dunford's innate good manners as their host, doing what he could to alleviate an incomprehensibly brittle atmosphere.

"I've just finished in *Major Barbara* at the Bristol Old Vic," Tess told him. "When I get back to London I start rehearsals for *School for Scandal.*"

"Really?" said Dunford. "Did you know that Sheridan was a regular visitor to Edenbridge? As a politician rather than a playwright though – the family were active Whigs in those days. We fell out with him over his opposition to the Combination Acts which outlawed trade unions. We have some very interesting letters of his from around that time. Perhaps you'd like to see them – in fact would you like to see round the house? I'd be very happy to show you."

Dunford was playing it very well, Maltravers felt, keeping up polite conversation in the teeth of Susan's silent aggression which was enveloping them all. The least he could do was respond to the invitation.

"That would be very enjoyable, but surely you have to attend to your other guests?"

"They'll be leaving soon. Please stay. It will be my pleasure." Dunford's obvious sincerity – even suggestion of eagerness – made it difficult to refuse him.

"Well, Gus and Tess might enjoy it, but we've been round the house dozens of times." Susan's tone implied further unwarranted criticism of Dunford, as though a private tour escorted by the heir to Edenbridge was faintly boring. "You two can stay if you want, but Peter and I are going home."

She looked at Dunford almost defiantly and Peter glanced at her sharply, bewildered at her behaviour and conscious of her bad manners.

"It's not all that late," he said. "Surely we could stay for . . ."

"*Peter, I want to go home!*"

There was an embarrassed silence as Susan immediately appeared aware that something had come too near the surface.

As they all looked at her uncomfortably she pressed her lips together as though on the brink of bursting into tears.

"I'm sorry." Her voice was only just under control, then she walked hurriedly away, pushing her abdomen between the other guests like a galleon driven by a gusting wind. There was an awkward pause.

"You'd better go after her, Peter," Tess said quietly. "I think she must be tired."

"Yes, of course." Peter frowned in annoyance as he watched his wife make her way towards the doors. "I don't know what's the matter with her. This baby seems to have given her more trouble than Tim and Emma. I apologise for her."

"There's no need for that, Peter," Dunford demurred.

"Yes there is. She was bloody rude and she knows it. Anyway I'll take her home. I gave you a key for the side door, didn't I? Let yourselves in and I'll see you tomorrow . . . Goodnight, Simon."

"See you at the match," Dunford called after him as Peter walked away, then he turned and smiled at Tess and Maltravers. "That's not like Susan at all. Pre-natal tension I expect. I'm sure she'll be all right. Look, just let me speak to a couple of people then I'll be with you."

"If you're sure it's no trouble," Maltravers said.

"Not in the least. I like showing people my home. I won't be long. Do help yourselves to more wine."

Tess looked sceptical as Dunford crossed the room and approached the council chairman and his wife who were standing by the fireplace.

"Pre-natal tension," she repeated disbelievingly. "Of which there was not the slightest sign until he appeared. What do you think?"

"I can't start to guess, but it was bloody obvious whatever it was all about," said Maltravers. "The strange thing is that I thought they were good friends."

"That's what Peter told me on the way here," said Tess.

"They've known Simon more or less ever since they moved into Capley. Apparently he doesn't make a big thing about being a belted Earl, or whatever he is, and has a number of friends in Bellringer Street. Peter talked about him in exactly the same way he talks about you."

"And what did Susan say?"

"It didn't strike me at the time, but in fact she said nothing at all, which seems significant in the light of what's happened. It was as though she almost hated him."

"It certainly seemed strong enough for that," Maltravers acknowledged. "But my impression of him was of a perfectly nice guy. How did he strike you?"

"He's very attractive and . . ." Tess paused, considering. "And gallant, I think is the word . . . no, not quite that . . . courteous in a way you don't meet very often. There's something . . . Put it this way, I think I would like him the more I got to know him."

"Well, we'll find out more about him shortly. Come on, let's get another drink."

Nobody approached them as they waited for Dunford to return. They were unknown in Capley and the English sense of impropriety about talking to strangers meant they received nothing more than polite, uncertain smiles from those who passed near them, although occasional glances lingered on Tess as though trying to place her. They amused themselves by examining the contents of the gallery which included souvenirs of distinguished visitors to Edenbridge House over the previous century, an intriguing collection of leading members of the Liberal party mixed at random with the founding fathers of jazz. It must have been the only place in the world where signed photographs of Gladstone and Lloyd George appeared on the same table as Bix Beiderbecke and Jelly Roll Morton. As the last remaining guests trickled out of the gallery, Dunford joined them again.

"I assume you've looked round here, so I'll show you the

rest." They followed as he led them out of the far end of the gallery and along a high, panelled corridor.

"You know, I'm appallingly ignorant about your family," Maltravers confessed. "How far does the title go back?"

"To just after the Restoration," Dunford replied. "Samuel Hawkhurst was involved in the sale of Dunkirk back to the French after Charles II returned to the throne and is credited with negotiating a good deal. The King granted him the Earldom and the Edenbridge lands go with it. That was in 1663 and the house was completed about ten years later. We like to claim that Wren may have been involved in the design but frankly that's a bit hazy. We've certainly got an Inigo Jones fireplace though. Come on, we'll start in here."

For more than an hour, Maltravers and Tess were given a private and very personal view of a house drenched in art, exquisite furniture and unique artefacts of three hundred years in still noble rooms rich with seductive magnificence. On an oyster-shell walnut table stood a gift glittering crystal from George III; nearby were a pair of silver embossed duelling pistols, one of which had nearly ended the intemperate young life of a future Prime Minister. There were incredibly detailed miniatures by Henry Bone; a Goya portrait that would have been the prized centrepiece of an art gallery hung indifferently in a corridor; a jasperware vase fashioned by Wedgwood himself; sumptuous, mellow tapestries that covered entire walls; Chippendale bearing Sèvres; exquisite Florentine statu-ettes accompanying rare Chinese porcelain. From ornate ceilings, down lush curtains to polished oak floorboards and priceless carpets, taste and history held conference in colours faded pale by time that could be measured in generations. And as he escorted them round, knowledgeable about everything he showed them, Dunford's affection for it all became increasingly apparent.

"Do you ever tire of all this?" Tess gestured helplessly round the ivory and old gold perfection of the morning room.

"Never," Dunford replied simply. "We may have to share it with the tourists now, but this happens to be my home. Come here."

He took her hand and led her to the edge of a long, sage green curtain which he took in his hand and softly rubbed it against her cheek.

"That's 200-year-old velvet," he said. "Would *you* tire of something as beautiful as that?"

Tess smiled and shook her head. "It feels like moleskin. But who are you going to ask to share it with you one day? Peter mentioned to me that you aren't married yet."

Dunford let go of the curtain and turned away unnecessarily to arrange it back into place.

"We'll have to see," he replied. "As you say, there's no Lady Dunford yet. Perhaps you're available, Miss Davy?" He looked back at Tess, part-quizzical, part-amused.

"Oh, that's awfully tempting, but I'm afraid not." For a moment they both looked at each other and then laughed. Standing on the other side of the room examining a pair of enamelled French watches, Maltravers glanced at them both with interest. Dunford's joking mild flirtation did not concern him, but he was intrigued by something he had caught in his voice when he had said there was no Lady Dunford. There had been the slightest undertones, so subtle that Maltravers had not been able to identify them with certainty. Melancholy? Regret? Apprehension? The moment vanished as swiftly as it had appeared, but left traces of curiosity in his mind.

"Anyway, that's about everything," Dunford said. "The only part you haven't seen are the family residential quarters in the West wing, but frankly they're rather modern and boring."

"What about Tom Bostock?" Maltravers asked, gently replacing one of the watches on its stand. "We only learned about him this afternoon, but I'd hate to miss him before he's buried."

"The family bastard? I'd forgotten him. I'll take you out through the cellars where we keep him."

"Do you agree with your mother?" Maltravers asked as Dunford led them out of the morning room and down some back stairs into a narrow, stone-flagged corridor. "I understand it's her wish that he should be buried after all this time."

"Absolutely," said Dunford. "I don't think we've behaved all that well towards old Tom, however big a villain he was. He did nothing more than cause the family some temporary embarrassment – and after all he couldn't help being the bastard son of the third Earl. Wishing him eternal damnation then cashing in on his remains seems excessive. If he did disgrace the family name, I think he's paid his debt now."

"Do you know much about him?" asked Tess.

"Not a great deal. Highwaymen were fairly commonplace around that time of course and there was nothing special about him. We've got an exhibition down here, based on what we've been able to find out, which includes a broadsheet about his execution complete with a contemporary illustration. Several people have said he looked rather like me. Anyway, you can see for yourselves."

He opened a door at the end of the passage and they entered the wide, low cellar at the far end of which stood a plain wooden coffin resting on trestles behind a red rope looped between metal poles. Dunford turned on the lights.

"When you consider all there is to see in Edenbridge House, it's ridiculous that this is so popular," he commented as they crossed the room. "However, in a few weeks . . . hell's teeth! Where is he?" He froze like a statue as they reached the rope.

"Perhaps he pops out for a drink on Friday nights," Maltravers suggested as all three of them gazed into the completely empty coffin.

Chapter Three

The sketch of the execution of Tom Bostock was sickening. Around the focal point of the gibbet and its victim surged a sea of Hogarthian features, feverish with brutal frenzy, jeering at the sight of the highwayman's grotesquely distorted face as life was agonisingly throttled out of him. Maltravers examined the observations of the unknown artist with grim interest. A plump young child, held up by its father to see better, pointing in fascinated and innocent delight at the dangling puppet of a dying man; a cleric looking as pitiless as a torturer; a pickpocket removing the watch from the embroidered waistcoat round the brandy-glass belly of a fat, engrossed and self-righteous nobleman; a mother suckling her baby; a boy cruelly and ignorantly mocking a human being's violent death throes by holding his neckerchief above his head and sticking his tongue out crookedly; helpless in the crowd, just one woman – Bostock's mistress perhaps – bowed in weeping despair, her hands clasped over her eyes. Maltravers sourly approved the small detail in the bottom corner where a cat and a dog sat at a small table drinking sherry; they were not the animals in Capley Market Square that day.

"And when the House of Commons debated bringing back capital punishment, one MP said he was prepared to be the hangman," he remarked drily. "I imagine if he had his way, he'd go the whole hog and show it on peak-time television. And he'd get a bloody audience."

He turned in distaste from the picture, part of the Tom Bostock exhibition which covered two walls of the cellar, and walked back to examine the unoccupied coffin again.

33

"It must be a joke," said Tess. "Who on earth would want to steal a skeleton?"

"Impoverished medical student perhaps?" suggested Maltravers, peering closely into the empty box to see if anything was available for a little amateur detection. "Apart from that slender possibility, it's a very uncommon case of common larceny."

They were alone with the mystery, Dunford having asked them to wait while he went to find Alister York, whose secretarial duties to Lord Pembury included security matters at Edenbridge House.

"What's equally incomprehensible is how somebody got away with it," Maltravers continued. "I can imagine some of the things we've seen this evening vanishing into pockets and handbags, but someone walking out of Edenbridge House with a full-size skeleton under their arm would presumably have been asked to explain themselves."

There was a sound of approaching footsteps along the stone-flagged corridor outside and Dunford reappeared through the door followed by Alister York. The secretary was a formidably large man with thick, wiry black hair and extraordinarily deep violet eyes set in a face tanned and creased like weathered leather. He was naturally stern, professionally correct and now looked concerned. Somewhat academically he crossed the cellar and looked into the coffin for himself.

"When did you last see him, Alister?" Dunford asked.

"Not for some days." The voice was as dark as the man, bass notes on a bassoon. "I don't come down here that often. However there was no guide on duty in here today."

"Why not?" Dunford snapped.

"Three of the guides were off ill and four extra coachloads of tourists arrived unexpectedly," York explained. "I had to make emergency arrangements and took . . . what's his name? . . . Humphreys out of here to show some of them round the house."

34

"So people were wandering around here unsupervised?" said Dunford.

"From about two o'clock, yes." York was meeting Dunford's clear annoyance with a catalogue of circumstances beyond his control. Maltravers gained the distinct feeling that the secretary did not like being reprimanded, the sort of man who would carefully cover all his actions so that if anything later went wrong he would have all his answers ready – and if necessary be able to blame someone else.

"I was just wondering how whoever it was got away with it."

Maltravers did not like the glare York shot at him as he spoke, as though he was interrupting some conversation which did not concern him. He bounced back the look with a slightly contemptuous expression, underlining the fact that he was Dunford's guest and York was his employee before continuing. "I can't understand how nobody noticed them."

The secretary hesitated before replying, as though resisting the inclination to tell Maltravers to mind his own damned business, then apparently deciding that his presence in the cellar had some connection with Dunford.

"Visitors arrive with all sorts of containers," he said, like an adult impatiently explaining something to a dull-witted child. "Full-sized rucksacks are not uncommon – as you would know if you had anything to do with the house. I trust that answers your question."

"Perfectly . . . thank you." Maltravers said with over-emphasised politeness, reflecting that Alister York was a man remarkably easy to dislike on short acquaintance.

"Do you wish me to call the police, Lord Dunford?" York asked.

"Pardon? No, not yet." Dunford shook his head as he thought. "The publicity will do us no good at all. It's almost certainly some ridiculous joke. Make inquiries among the house staff and the guides but tell them they are not to say anything. And check with the coach operators who were here today to see if it's turned up in one of their seats . . . Have you a key for this room?"

"Not with me, but there's one in the office. We don't usually keep it locked."

"Well, lock it now," Dunford instructed then turned to Tess and Maltravers. "I must go and tell Lord Pembury about this, but I'll see you out first."

All of them went back upstairs to the main entrance hall where York went into his office to collect the cellar door key and Dunford let his visitors out through the huge front door: great panels of oak studded with iron heads of nails the size of crown pieces.

"May I ask you to keep this to yourselves for the time being?" he asked.

"Of course," Maltravers agreed. "Although if Bostock doesn't turn up pretty sharpish, won't you have some difficulty in keeping it quiet? You'll have more tourists arriving tomorrow expecting to see him."

"We'll keep the cellar closed and put them off somehow," said Dunford. "There'll be complaints, but we can handle that." He held out his hand. "It's been a great pleasure meeting you both. I'm sorry we haven't had the opportunity to talk more about your career, Miss Davy. Perhaps we'll be able to at the party after the match tomorrow? I'll see you then."

"Thank you for showing us your home," said Maltravers. "It was fascinating, even without the disappearing skeleton. Incidentally, how do we get out of the park at this time of night?"

"There's a small door with a Yale lock cut into the Bellringer Street gate," said Dunford. "Just make sure it's secure behind you."

He smiled and closed the great door, leaving them at the top of the wide semicircle of steps that fell like the train of a gown from the terrace on to the gravelled drive. Residual luminescence from the vanished sun washed the night sky with mother-of-pearl, with silhouettes of pipistrelle bats flickering across it, their high-pitched squeaks the only sound in the gloaming stillness.

"Interesting evening," Maltravers remarked as they walked away from the silent purple-shadowed mass of the house, footsteps on the crisp foam of the gravel path loud in the silence. "I thought body snatching went out with Burke and Hare."

"That's just a stupid joke," Tess said dismissively. "What was much more interesting was Susan's behaviour when Simon appeared. I still can't get over that."

"She certainly didn't make much effort to hide her feelings, whatever was causing them," Maltravers agreed. "Or perhaps they were so strong that she was unable to control them. Peter just looked confused about it. Anyway, unless she wants to talk about it, it's none of our business."

They passed under the arch of the Bellringer Street lodge through the door in the gate. From the top of the hill they could see the tangled skeins of orange street lights of the New Town, but Old Capley was dark under the stars, the drop of the street illuminated only by two pools of light cast by ancient lampposts. Just out of synchronisation, the clocks of St Barbara's church and Edenbridge House sent out twenty-four answering strokes to mark the hour. When they entered the Penroses' kitchen they found a note from Susan on the table.

"Sorry about tonight," they read. "I don't know what was the matter with me. You know where everything is if you want to make yourselves a drink. See you in the morning. Love, Susan."

"Are we back to pre-natal tension then?" asked Maltravers.

Tess looked at the handwriting, scribbled and agitated, a hasty and duty note of apology to explain away an embarrassing indiscretion.

"If Simon thinks I'm that simple, he's out of his tree," she replied caustically. "That was his explanation but don't ask me to believe it."

They went quietly upstairs and Maltravers was in bed reading when Tess returned from the bathroom.

"By the way," he said casually. "I gained the distinct impression that the heir to the Edenbridge millions was making a pass at you earlier this evening."

"Was he?" Tess smiled and blinked with exaggerated innocence. "Well, I'm afraid he's not the first one, darling. Do you mind?"

Maltravers looked back at her sardonically. "I see. The prospect of being the mistress of Edenbridge House appeals, does it?"

She stared at him for a moment then slipped her nightdress off her shoulders, letting it fall to the floor before climbing into the bed beside him.

"For an intelligent man, you can be amazingly stupid sometimes," she told him. "Come here."

Afterwards, as they lay half-awake, they heard footsteps of someone walking down the hill past the house, whistling softly; Alister York was going home.

"Now what the hell's happened?" demanded a mystified transatlantic voice. "The guy didn't even hit the goddamned ball and those little bits of wood are still standing up. Why's he out?"

"Lbw," Maltravers explained.

"L. B. who?"

"Leg before wicket. His leg stopped the ball hitting the stumps."

"I thought that was the general idea."

"It is, but you can't just stand there with your legs together to prevent it happening."

Milton Chambers II looked further confused. In the six months he had lived in England, occupying a house in Bellringer Street owned by the British satellite of a Philadelphia engineering company, his natural anglophilia had flourished. He had traced his family ancestry back to a village within a hundred miles of Boston Stump (virtually next door by

American standards) and the hallowed shades of the Pilgrim Fathers, and was now contemplating paying several thousand pounds to acquire the title of Lord of the Manor of Compton St Peter in Dorset, a distinction which would have allowed him to graze his sheep on the ancient Lord's Pasture had not the county council inconsiderately run the village bypass straight through it. But such efforts, he was convinced, would be seriously deficient unless he somehow managed to comprehend the curious summer game which obsessed the true Englishman. He knew what was *not* cricket – making a pass at another man's wife, cheating at cards in the club – but the rules and occult subtleties of the real thing eluded him. He was attending the Town v. Estate match in the manner of an eager novitiate and had attached himself to Maltravers, obviously an advanced expert.

"Legs together," he repeated. "Is that something to do with that maiden thing you were telling me about? Hell, I didn't realise sex came into this."

"A maiden is an over – that's six deliveries of the ball from either end – in which no runs are scored," Maltravers repeated patiently. "Lbw is something the batsman does wrong which means he is out. There is no sex in cricket."

"You said something about goolies," Chambers reminded him suspiciously.

"Googlies," Maltravers corrected firmly and hastily. "That's an off break delivered with an apparent leg break action or vice versa, like that chap just bowled. There is also a Chinaman which is an off break from a left-handed bowler to a right-handed batsman." He smiled at the American sympathetically. "But I don't think you're ready for that yet."

Chambers, who was finding the whole course of instruction as incomprehensible as Sanskrit, silently agreed. Maltravers privately recalled the story of the great Groucho Marx sitting in the Long Room at Lords having the game explained to him while a match was in progress. He showed a ready grasp of the basic principles then surveyed the proceedings for several minutes before demanding: "So when do they start?" Maltravers had experienced similar difficulties with the rules of American Football, a game which appeared to him to be some manner of semi-organised public riot.

"What's the score?" Chambers inquired; the combination of seemingly unrelated numbers on the scoreboard made no sense to him.

"Twenty-seven for one," Maltravers replied. "The two batsmen in now are Lord Dunford and Alister York, who are the best in the side, so we ought to start seeing some action."

"What about you?" Chambers asked, convinced that anyone who could talk about the game so expertly must be a gifted player as well.

"Merely a replacement brought in at the last moment," Maltravers said dismissively. "With a bit of luck, I won't even be called upon to bat."

Maltravers had felt it polite to offer to go in at number eleven, hoping to avoid having to do very much. The tension round the waistband of his white flannels was a permanent reminder that several summers had bloomed and faded since he had last played. As he stretched out in a deckchair under the mottled shade of a copper beech tree, Tess lay face down on the grass beside him, absorbed in a book. When she had first fallen in love with Maltravers, she had wanted to show an interest in all his passions and had spent an entire day with him at the Oval suffering a rising sense of total disbelief. When told that the proceedings would continue for another two whole days – and already looked like ending in a draw – she had smiled nervously and announced that she really had to go and see her aunt in Broadstairs. Maltravers later discovered that such duty visits were only marginally less disagreeable to her than cleaning the oven and had drawn his own conclusions. Even the prevailing circumstances of a blazing Saturday afternoon and an almost lyrically perfect setting for the game – wide swathe of smooth grass against a backdrop of variegated jade trees with the square tower of the parish church peeping above – were not enough to engage her attention.

Accompanied by the drowsy chatter of the spectators, Dunford and York settled down to build the foundations of a decent score and for a quarter of an hour garnered runs almost as they pleased. Then York rashly slashed at a delivery turning away from him, clipping it into the grateful hands of first slip (a piece of field-placing terminology which had caused Chambers much fascination) who had been placed there precisely for such an indiscretion.

"Silly bugger," someone sitting near them remarked feelingly. "He should have left it alone."

York appeared to share the same opinion, pulling his gloves off angrily as he left the wicket and hurling his bat to the ground by the boundary rope before walking away. Out in the field, the Town captain encouraged his side with shouts and handclaps; all he had to do now was keep the bowling away from the experienced Dunford and pick off the rest of the side like a sniper. Maltravers watched gloomily as wicket after wicket fell to the most hapless of batting. He buckled on his pads as number nine went in and survived only three balls; number ten, a petrified, pimply youth, was clean bowled by the next delivery, his stumps splayed out like a broken fan, and Maltravers walked out with the bowler on a hat trick to finish the Estate innings. As he reached the wicket, Dunford strolled across and spoke to him.

"Two balls left in this over," he said. "Try and block him and I'll keep strike after that."

Maltravers nodded, then went to the striker's end and took guard, casually glancing round as the field moved in like wolves on wounded prey. Twenty yards beyond the opposite stumps, the Town's pace bowler polished the ball on his flannels with quiet, deliberate menace. Maltravers settled, tapping the end of his bat softly on the ground and looked straight at him as he thundered in.

Anyone who thinks cricket is a slow game should experience facing a fast bowler in full cry. No sooner do you see his arm arcing through his delivery action a mere twenty-two yards away, than a very hard missile is suddenly in your immediate neighbourhood, unnervingly hissing past your head if the pitch is firm and the bowler is in an unfriendly frame of mind. Not that anything so hostile as a bouncer was called for on this occasion; on a hat-trick, confident that the final Estate batsman would prove as incompetent as his predecessors, the bowler felt that simple speed and accuracy on middle stump would be elementary overkill. Dunford looked uneasy as he raced in. He was a bare couple of paces short of releasing the ball when Maltravers dropped his bat and turned away, clasping a gloved hand to his face.

"Sorry!" he shouted.

Thrown off momentum, the bowler lost his direction and the ball streaked harmlessly through to the wicketkeeper as Maltravers tugged out a handkerchief and applied it to his eye which contained nothing more than a wicked glint. Dunford suddenly found the face of his bat strangely interesting. The bowler glared down the pitch as Maltravers replaced the handkerchief, retrieved his bat and waved an apologetic acknowledgment.

"All right," he called down the pitch. "Sorry about that."

As their bowler stalked back to his mark, the Town fielders exchanged suspicious glances; Maltravers had either bottled out or used an old trick of gamesmanship (the morals of cricket were sometimes not quite so squeaky clean as Chambers felt them to be). But it would not work a second time – and the hat-trick was still on. Even Tess, who had condescended to watch while Maltravers was batting, could sense the gathered hostility now concentrating on his tall, tense figure.

By any standards, the next delivery was an excellent one, hurled at maximum speed, low and laser straight on Maltravers' stumps. Jerking up his right elbow as he stretched forward, he met it with the full face of his bat and it bounced harmlessly into the covers. The Town side deflated with disappointment as Dunford looked at Maltravers then turned away, intrigued and slightly surprised.

Furious at being thwarted, the bowler failed to notice what Dunford had seen; Maltravers' classic forward defensive stroke had revealed an unexpected touch of real quality. The final ball of the over had a fatal additional anger about it which flawed its control, causing it to turn just fractionally to leg. Maltravers stepped smoothly back and right and whipped the blade of his bat at it, hooking it viciously straight at the head of short square leg, who dropped to the ground, seemingly determined to examine the grass at his feet as closely as possible. Maltravers' caustic nod at him as he straightened up and the streaking ball banged against the metal scoreboard, the umpire somewhat academically signalling a four, advised him to find a safer place to stand. As the field changed over, the Town side looking at Maltravers guardedly, Dunford walked down the wicket and spoke to him again.

"As captain of this side, I must formally reprimand you for your trickery with that first ball," he said, poker-faced. "However, I also want to know what the hell you're doing coming in at number eleven."

"I'm only a guest player," Maltravers reminded him. "It seemed discourteous to go in ahead of the regular team members."

"Well, it's a relief to have you here at last." Dunford glanced across at the scoreboard. "Eighty-three with nine overs left. Let's see if we can top the hundred, shall we? They've got to bring their spinners back in a couple of overs which will help."

In the following hectic three quarters of an hour, the final fifty-four balls produced a further hundred and twenty runs, the spectators cheering constantly as the two men mercilessly slaughtered the bowling, skilfully altering their tactics to outwit the permutations of defensive fieldings tried by the increasing

43

frantic Town captain. Maltravers considerately took only a single off the penultimate delivery, allowing Dunford the pleasure of cavalierly leaping down the pitch to meet the final ball, bat swinging like a broadsword, to send it soaring back over the dejected bowler's head for a last, satisfying six. As the Town side joined the applause rattling all around, Dunford threw his arm round Maltravers' shoulders as they walked off.

"Not one for the purists, but bloody marvellous!" he exclaimed. "All right, where did you learn to bat like that?"

"My father," Maltravers replied with a nostalgic smile. "He got his cricket Blue at Oxford as well and turned out for the Gentlemen against the Players a couple of times. But frankly I'm out of practice."

Dunford nodded in agreement. "You were damned lucky with a couple of those square cuts. Anyway, you've given us the first chance of winning this match that we've had for years. You've earned a beer."

They joined the rest of the players at the trestle tables bearing barrels and sandwiches, which had been set up under the trees.

"Any news about the skeleton?" Maltravers asked quietly as they turned away with their drinks. Dunford shook his head as he lowered his face towards the sun-sparkling foam bubbling over the rim of his glass.

"Not a thing," he replied, withdrawing from the froth and wiping his mouth with the back of his hand. "None of the guides saw anything and, as you know, it was not the most organised of days. We've contacted various coach operators, but no luck there either."

"So are you going to tell the police now?"

"Not yet," said Dunford. "We're still taking the view that it's just some sort of joke and he'll turn up fairly soon."

"Do you think anyone might demand a ransom for him?" Maltravers asked unexpectedly. Dunford stared at him in amazement.

"What an extraordinary idea . . . still, I expect it's just

possible. After all, someone stole poor old Charlie Chaplin from his grave for the same reason, didn't they? But I can't see it. My father would be very disinclined to pay money to get Tom Bostock back."

"But Lady Pembury might think differently," Maltravers observed. "As I understand it, she feels it's a matter of family honour that Tom Bostock should be properly buried. That could be a persuasive point if he's been . . ." He frowned briefly. "Is kidnapped the right word in this situation?"

Dunford looked at him thoughtfully for a moment.

"You know, you may have a point," he said finally, then shook his head in immediate rejection. "But it's ridiculous. At the moment not all that many people know what was being planned about the funeral, and I can't accept that any of them would do what you're suggesting. The trouble with you is that you've got the hyperactive imagination of a writer."

"I've also got the experience of a journalist," Maltravers added. "And that taught me there are few things – however bizarre – that somebody will not actually do."

"We'll see," said Dunford. "In the meantime, I'd still like you to keep it to yourself. It may leak out eventually, but we'd much rather keep it quiet and hope that he just turns up again. Excuse me, I must go and talk to the visiting captain."

As Dunford walked away, Maltravers became aware of someone hovering at his side. He turned to see a young woman, strikingly like a pretty, timid bird, offering him a plate of sandwiches.

"Would you like one of these?" She sounded very apprehensive about making the offer.

"How very kind," he replied. "I didn't expect to be waited on."

The girl – he had instantly decided it was unsuitable to describe her as a woman although she appeared to be in her mid-twenties – smiled nervously and raised the plate towards him like a frightened acolyte serving the High Priest. He took a

45

sandwich and she scuttled away before he had time to say anything more, leaving him with an impression of crucifying shyness.

"Hell, that was more like it!"

The enthusiastic voice of Milton Chambers II burst in upon Maltravers again like a man who has just seen the Grand Canyon for the first time. "You and Lord Dunford really took 'em to the cleaners. Is it always like that? Kinda slow at the start and all the action at the end?"

"Limited over games usually are," Maltravers admitted. Chambers grinned at him crudely.

"And you tell me cricket's got nothing to do with sex? Come on."

"Mr Chambers, that is heresy and if you repeat it, I must warn you that we'll have to come over and take Yorktown back," Maltravers told him sternly. "The great thing to remember about cricket is that it is not a game. It is a morality."

"Ignore him, Mr Chambers." Tess had joined them with Peter and Susan. "Gus is insufferable when he gets pompous. Shut up, darling, and eat your sandwich."

"And very good it is," said Maltravers, cheerfully unabashed. He had reached the happy stage of life where embarrassment over his actions was a youthful memory. "Although I can't imagine why the young lady who gave it me seemed terrified that I was going to bite her."

"Small girl, china-doll face, long black hair, wearing a yellow dress?" Susan inquired. Maltravers nodded in some surprise through a mouthful of asparagus rolled in brown bread. "I thought so. Joanna York. God, I want to shake her sometimes."

"Alister York's wife," Peter explained. "You've met him of course."

"Yes, last night after you left." Maltravers had not felt it necessary to observe Dunford's request to keep the disappearance of Tom Bostock secret to the extent of not telling his hosts. "Anyway, why do you want to shake her?"

"She's so . . . obedient." Susan sounded exasperated. "It's unreal the way she just obeys Alister like a child. She's a poppet when you get to know her but she makes me furious."

"Funny thing marriage," Maltravers remarked. "Some women like being treated that way."

"Well I like to think that one day she'll learn better," said Susan. "It's grotesque. She's the only woman I know who doesn't breathe a word of criticism against her husband, even when she's with a group of other wives. It's as though she can't even talk without his permission."

Further comments on Joanna York were prevented by Dunford returning to introduce Lord and Lady Pembury, who had been watching the match from garden chairs set up beneath a canvas sun umbrella. They were accompanied by a man Maltravers did not recognise but whose looks suggested a possible relative.

"A splendid innings, Mr Maltravers," Pembury said as they shook hands.

The twelfth Earl's manner was bone-deep aristocracy; centuries at the heart of the English establishment creating a demeanour of tangible polite condescension to the lower orders of society, which in his case began with the viscounts. Repeated marriages within a limited circle had laid down the family's anaemic looks; the blood may have been of the deepest blue, but was probably insipid. He and his wife resembled fine Dresden figures, their delicate physiques reflected in both Dunford and the stranger.

"I just can't understand Alister," Pembury continued. "Most unlike him to play a shot like that. Where is he by the way?"

Everyone instinctively looked round as if Pembury's inquiry about the whereabouts of his secretary carried the implied instruction to find him; the legacy of generations of having orders obeyed without question.

"I saw him walking back towards the house after he was out," said Peter. "Probably checking that everything was all right."

47

As the absent York was forgotten, Maltravers observed the young man with the Pemburys, dressed in a smooth, cream linen suit with a mustard-coloured silk handkerchief erupting out of the top pocket. He gave the impression of being totally bored by everything and everyone around him.

"Oh, this is my cousin Oliver Hawkhurst," Dunford said. "Oliver, Augustus Maltravers. The writer."

"Really?"

Maltravers rarely made snap judgements of people, particularly on the evidence of only one word, but he was prepared to make an exception in this case. Hawkhurst had managed to inject disinterest, superciliousness and even a slice of contempt into his reply, and seemed to think that even looking at Maltravers was really too much trouble. Dunford had caught the unmistakable tone and glared at his cousin in undisguised annoyance.

"A distant cousin?" Maltravers inquired mildly, which was as far as he could go in the circumstances, but he had the satisfaction of seeing Hawkhurst's sneering face flush with anger before turning away. Dunford grinned and appeared to appreciate the implied insult.

Hawkhurst remained with his back turned as Lord and Lady Pembury talked to Susan about the baby – it struck Maltravers that she seemed unusually reluctant to discuss the subject and wondered why – and Milton Chambers appeared momentarily uncertain as to whether a potential Lord of the Manor should bow when introduced to a Peer of the Realm and the correct form of address consistent with a great republican heritage. After a few minutes, Dunford and Maltravers left the group as the match restarted.

"I'm afraid cousin Oliver showed his usual charming manners just now," Dunford remarked as they followed the umpires out. "He's like that with most people and I find it offensive. I liked your return of service though – that got up his snotty little nose."

Maltravers found the remark revealing; in a family like the

Pemburys, whose tribal loyalty would rival that of a Mafia clan, overt criticism of a member, especially to a stranger, was almost unknown. Obviously Dunford had very little time for this particular relation.

"Is he really a distant cousin?" he asked.

"Far from it. After me he's the heir to Edenbridge. He's making one of his regular visits to see how I am. It always disappoints him to discover that I haven't contracted something fatal. Cousin Oliver has an unhealthy desire to get hold of this place and turn it into some appalling Disneyland . . . Anyway, enough of him. Are you a bowler as well?"

"No, I am not," Maltravers said firmly. "Stick me out on the boundary where I won't do any harm."

Dispirited by the score amassed against them, the Town side put up a feeble resistance. Alister York made up for his earlier batting error with a thirty-yard throw of pinpoint accuracy to run out their opening batsman and Maltravers amazed himself by taking a flying one-handed catch just inside the boundary rope, falling backwards and thumping to the ground just in front of Tess in the process.

"Remember your age, darling," she called out. Maltravers scowled at her.

The Town's innings closed more than a hundred short of their target and Dunford led his side off to the delighted applause of the spectators, only the more elderly of whom could remember the Estate's last victory in the fixture. As the Estate side celebrated their success with the remains of the beer, an odd incident marred the atmosphere when an irate tourist appeared in their midst demanding to see Lord Pembury who had, in fact, left immediately the game had finished.

"We want our money back," he demanded, loudly enough for everyone over a wide distance to hear him. "It's bloody disgusting, scaring little children out of their wits."

"Excuse me," Dunford murmured, replacing his glass on the table. "I'd better see what all this is about."

49

He went across to the man, skinny and aggressive with a good deal of pink perspiring flesh protruding from short-sleeved shirt and Empire-builder shorts.

"Perhaps I can help," he said courteously. "I'm sorry that Lord Pembury isn't here, but I'm Lord Dunford."

The aggrieved paying customer looked slightly uncertain for a moment; asking for someone with a title was one thing, being suddenly confronted with one appeared to be quite another.

"It's your ghost," he said grumpily. "Frightened the life out of our Sue-Ellen."

Maltravers added the child's name to his personal collection of Darrens, Waynes and Jasons who seemed to inhabit his local supermarket. Spawned, named and dressed out of the television age and with ice cream now occupying a fair proportion of her singularly plain face, she seemed totally recovered from whatever had happened to her.

"There is no ghost in Edenbridge House," Dunford assured her father. "I don't know what your little girl . . ."

"Are you calling me a liar?" The mildest suggestion of contradiction had instantly rekindled the tourist's wrath. "We found her screaming the place down."

"Where was this exactly?" Dunford asked.

"Over there." The man pointed irritatedly to the West wing of the house. "Anyway, it doesn't matter where it happened."

"But those are the private family quarters," said Dunford. "They're not open to the public. How on earth did your child get in there?"

"It doesn't matter." The man remained pugnacious, although now possibly apprehensive that his child may have trespassed where she was forbidden. "We heard her screaming and found her crying in a corridor." He decided to support a suddenly shaky case with a second line of protest. "We'd already complained when they said the cellar where you keep the skeleton was closed. That was the main reason for coming here. Sue-Ellen was looking forward to that."

The party, never stout in the first place, was collapsing rapidly and visibly. His announcement of Sue-Ellen's morbid juvenile hopes sounded almost pleading.

"Well, I can only suggest that she may have seen a member of the household staff," said Dunford. "If that terrified her, it seems best that she did not see a human skeleton. I'm sorry if she was frightened, but it really must be your responsibility to look after your own child."

Surrounded by witnesses to his own confession that he had been in the wrong in letting his daughter wander unsupervised around the house and his argument about not seeing Tom Bostock turned back on him, the tourist gave instant indications of raising his level of protest to avoid humiliating retreat. Dunford hastily defused the situation.

"However," he added, as the man's face started to go through a spectrum of red as he remustered his aggression, "in the circumstances, perhaps your little girl would like a doll from our tourists' shop. With our compliments of course. Perhaps that will make her feel better."

The rush of blood spontaneously dissipated into a reluctant grunt of acceptance.

"Right then. Who do we see?"

"This gentleman will take care of it." Dunford gestured to York who was standing nearby. "Alister, will you take this lady and gentleman and their little girl to the shop, please? I think she would like one of our Victorian-style dolls."

People looked away, hiding their amusement as the little man kept what tattered dignity he could in outmanoeuvred retreat.

"God preserve us from the British public," Dunford said feelingly as he rejoined Maltravers and Tess. "Well, at least it will get rid of one of those hideous mock-Victorian monstrosities that no one will buy."

"What do you think she saw?" Maltravers wondered.

"Certainly not a ghost," Dunford replied firmly. "That is one thing Edenbridge House doesn't have. Not even Tom

Bostock haunts the place and he's got more reason to than anyone."

"Well, she'd have terrified any ghost with that scream," Tess remarked as Sue-Ellen's screech comfortably crossed the increasing distance between them. "I wonder what brought it on again?"

Sue-Ellen, infant and inarticulate, was screaming in terror at the tall, forbidding man who was walking in front of her father.

"I trust you'll be at the party tonight," Dunford said to Maltravers as they walked away from the cricket pitch with the Penroses.

"We're told it's part of the traditions of the match," he replied. "Where is it again?"

"Trevor and Evelyn Darby's, the enormous house just over the road from us," said Peter. "Trevor's President of the Town club. It usually goes on until breakfast time for those who can last the pace."

"What about you?" Dunford gestured towards Susan's body hesitantly, as though somehow embarrassed at the evidence of her advanced pregnancy.

"Oh yes, we'll be there, Simon." She looked down at herself ruefully. "Although this year I think I'll be leaving early."

Maltravers noticed that Dunford seemed somehow relieved. It was unlikely that it was because Peter and Susan would be at the party; more likely he was grateful that there had been no repetition of her inexplicable behaviour towards him at the concert the previous evening.

"Marvellous, I'll look forward to . . ." Dunford stopped suddenly, his eyes flashing towards a white MG, driving through the crowds in the park rather too fast and noisily dropping a gear before sweeping round the side of Edenbridge House towards the family's private entrance. His face hardened and for a moment it was as if nobody else was there, then he turned to them again.

"Anyway, I must be getting back. I've got a great deal to do. See you all later."

It was not, Maltravers reflected, the politest of withdrawals as Dunford turned abruptly and walked swiftly towards the house. Despite the heat of the day, the MG had not had its roof down and Maltravers had been unable to see who had been driving it, but he or she was clearly not a welcome visitor as far as Dunford was concerned. Watching Dunford go, Susan felt a sense of relief that she had managed to speak to him normally; she was still furious with herself for allowing things to come so dangerously near the surface when he had unexpectedly appeared after the concert. Dunford's mind was filled with the anticipated difficulties of an angry and emotional encounter with his lover.

Chapter Four

While it did not immediately appear to be one, Old Capley had in many ways reverted to its original existence as a village. Distinctly separated from the New Town by the railway line to London and what had at one time been part of the Great North Road, it had become an official Conservation Area, clustered about the skirts of St Barbara's which floated high above its rooftops. There was a village gossip, a drunk, even at one time the scandalous suggestion of a local whore, several candidates for the position of resident idiot and a yearly pattern of events around which the social calendar revolved: the Spring Flower Festival at the church, the Conservative Party Summer Dance, Autumn Fair and Christmas Bazaar for the deserving poor of the parish. There was also Trevor and Evelyn Darby's annual party after the Town v. Estate cricket match which, in its time, had achieved its own legends. At least four marriages, several affairs and two divorces could be traced back to it and an impromptu inebriated attempt at Kent Treble Bobs on the church bells still lived in the memory, as unforgettably as it had once clangingly disturbed the peace at three o'clock in the morning. But this was to be the last party before Trevor Darby took up the position of chief executive of a multinational bank in Saudi Arabia where the average account exceeded the gross domestic product of several Third World countries. Floated on a tidal wave of alcohol and with enough food to solve Oxfam's global problems for a week, the evening was calculated to strip away all normal inhibitions of English reserve and leave a legacy of thundering hangovers and vague misgivings of half-remembered indiscretions.

When Maltravers and Tess arrived with Peter and Susan shortly before nine o'clock, nearly a hundred fully paid-up members of the middle classes were concerned with nothing more than endless discussion of their concerns. As they stepped through the front door, the seething clamour of talk was like a curtain of sound blown into their faces.

"Nine hundred overdrawn and this snotty letter arrives from the manager" . . . *"For God's sake, I found contraceptive pills in her bedroom. She's only fifteen"* . . . *"You can't just say that bringing back National Service will solve everything"* . . . *"Then he had the nerve to say he'd bring the union in"* . . . *"Of course we feel guilty about it, but comprehensive schools just haven't worked. The fees go up again next term as well."*

Weaving like a barrage balloon with faulty controls, Susan was led through to a chair by Evelyn Darby as Peter and Maltravers were joined by some members of the Estate team. Tess stood next to them, irritatedly sipping her first glass of wine too quickly, wondering if it was possible to escape the wretched game anywhere in the house. Surrounding them on the walls of the large square hall immediately inside the front door were photographs of teams long past, statically posed Victorians in moustaches and sepia, the ruffled casualness of the 1930s, the slick Brylcreemed hair of the post-war years. There were framed cartoons of famous players with immense heads on diminutive bodies; an ancient, scarred bat treasured in a long glass case; the county cap won by Darby's father. Listening to incomprehensible references to leg glances and sticky wickets, Tess looked for any avenue of relief. Strangers regarded her with discreet uncertainty, half recognising the face but either unable to place her or hesitant to approach. She was considering going up to a couple obviously engaged in an excited "Do you know who that is? I'm sure it's . . . wasn't she in . . . you know, with that chap who was in the other thing?" discussion when the front door opened again and Dunford walked in with

55

his cousin Oliver and a man Tess did not know. As Trevor Darby welcomed them, Dunford smiled at her and she noticed his eyes flashed approvingly up and down her soft green, flowing dress. It was the sort of look with which she was very familiar and was usually followed by a pulling-in of stomachs, a casual discarding of inconvenient wives and a familiarity with little-known but excellent restaurants in town should she ever be free for a quiet dinner with adultery for dessert. The couple, who had just decided to approach her under the impression that she was someone else entirely, looked disappointed as Dunford stepped across the hall and joined her.

"Good evening, Miss Davy. May I say that you look very lovely?"

"Thank you, kind sir." Tess gave a slight bogus bow and returned his look equivocally. She was amused, but instinctively cautious.

"Let me introduce Luke Norman." Dunford half turned towards the stranger. "He runs an antique shop in Richmond in which I have an interest. Luke . . . well, I don't think I need explain who Tess Davy is."

"Of course not. Simon said you would be here. It's a great pleasure to meet you."

Tess later wondered why she had not realised certain things at that moment. Luke Norman was . . . the only word that came to her was beautiful. Black hair, pewter-grey eyes with a natural grace about his movements and the very way he stood. At one time she could have been very foolish about a man with such looks. Please don't be a cricketer, she thought – and say something else, I like your voice.

"Simon was telling me that you're a friend of Gus Maltravers, the writer."

"Yes, he's . . ." Tess turned to where Maltravers had been standing next to her, but he had wandered across the hall with Peter and the other men to examine some photographs on the wall. She sighed. "I'm afraid he's talking cricket at the moment."

"There's a lot of it about," Norman observed mordantly, glancing round the hall. "Personally, I've detested the game ever since they made me play it at school."

Tess smiled in consoled gratitude. "You I like. I've had the damned game inflicted on me all day. You weren't at the match were you?"

"No, but I gather they won."

"Yes. Gus has been talking about nothing else since."

"Simon's been virtually the same," said Norman as a fellow sufferer, glancing at Dunford. "We'll have to make sure they both . . . behave this evening."

The simultaneous arrival of someone with a tray of drinks and Maltravers' return covered the slight edge in Norman's voice which Tess caught but did not hold for long enough to think about. The four of them started to chat about antiques, including some of the treasures of Edenbridge House, while the barrage of talk rolled on around them.

"But the gypsies have got to live somewhere" . . . *"Of course he won't be prosecuted because he's a member of the Cabinet"* . . . *"Then I decided to try the five iron"* . . . *"I used lumpfish roe and honestly you can't tell the difference."*

Alister York's mask of cold politeness covered his contempt for Oliver Hawkhurst as he diplomatically avoided revealing anything to him about the affairs of Edenbridge House, suggesting that certain questions could only be dealt with by Lord Pembury personally. It indicated the extent of Hawkhurst's financial crisis – York knew all about the imminent collapse of the property company and the bailiff's notice on the door of the ludicrous nightclub – that he would probe the possibilities of salvation by his uncle by approaching his secretary at the party. Edenbridge money had been provided in the past for previous boneheaded indiscretions but there would be no more. Lord Pembury had tetchily authorised the last

£60,000 a year earlier with a warning that any further commercial disasters his nephew created would be his own problem. Now Hawkhurst, who had blatantly used the Pembury connection to conjure up six-figure loans, appeared unable to grasp the situation. The merchant bankers, to whom he now scathingly referred as usurers, had become icy and hard-eyed, but Lord Pembury was indifferent about a member of the family appearing in the bankruptcy court. Hawkhurst had tried asking his cousin and his bitterness and resentment at being born just outside the charmed circle of family wealth had deepened to hatred when Dunford had also refused to help.

As he bit on the humiliation of having to approach York, the censorious and patronising secretary, in a last desperate effort to extract something from the Pembury wealth, Dunford walked past with Luke Norman and Tess and Maltravers. Seeing them disappear into the garden at the back of the house through the door of the crowded sitting room, Hawkhurst's hatred was fuelled by the ever-recurring thought of how agonisingly and impotently near he was to becoming heir to the title, the house, money and salvation. He frequently played out in his mind the scene where he would dangle that prospect in front of his persecutors, and watch them turn to fawning sycophants, prurient at the prospect of the smallest fraction of one of the greatest fortunes in England. But the dream was always destroyed by meeting the man who stood in his way; not yet thirty, depressingly healthy and surely soon to produce the wife and inevitable son, pushing Hawkhurst irreversibly down the line of inheritance, an embarrassing, impoverished and finally irrelevant and excluded relative.

York watched Dunford walk past as well, distastefully noting how he held Tess's arm as he guided her between the guests and out of the house. He had been planning to murder him for so long that further evidence of his casual liaisons with women was academic.

It was a long garden with high walls, stained by countless

changing seasons to a patchwork of old rose and rust brickwork.
Three steps led up from a paved terrace to the start of a lawn,
cut off towards the far end by a wooden trellis fence smothered
with Dorothy Perkins roses. Many of the guests had made their
way outside, the sound of their still-incessant voices drifting
upwards into the limpid lemon evening air.

"Isn't that a Vincent's tie?" Maltravers asked, nodding
towards Dunford as they walked up the steps.

"Yes. Not many people recognise it."

"Is it something special?" Tess looked at the pattern of small
gold crowns on a dark blue background.

"Oxford Blues – or those who get near enough – can wear
them," Maltravers explained. "My father got one for cricket as
well. The Cambridge equivalent is the Hawks tie, which . . ."

Tess's smile coupled excessive sweetness with incipient
insanity and she used his full first name, a standard sign that
their relationship was not working at that moment.

"Augustus, if you mention that bloody game again, I am
going to throw up! Right?"

Dunford laughed. "Then I'll rescue you from it. There are
people here who would love to meet you and I shall personally
hit anyone who uses the word. Come with me."

They merged with the guests ebbing through the garden and
the rooms of the house like water trickling between rocks,
accompanied by the racing torrent of talk.

*"Changed his tune of course when I told him I knew the Chief
Constable personally"* . . . *"Make it Tuesday and it's on my expenses"* . . . *"I don't know who he's screwing but if he gets Aids he'll get
no sympathy from me"* . . . *"Forty to the gallon on a long run."*

Tess was never quite sure how she found herself alone with
Dunford. For a couple of hours there had been a series of people
talking to her about her career, endless bottles of wine kept
appearing and there was a well-mannered mêlée around the

food tables. Back in the hall, Dunford introduced Norman to a man who wanted to buy some Regency glassware and Maltravers had been pinned in a corner by a woman who did a "little modest writing" and wanted to know what motivated a true professional; she was quite disillusioned when he said money. The flashing lights and throbbing rhythms of a disco completed the disintegration of polite behaviour loosened by alcohol, and people grouped and regrouped constantly. Dunford asked Tess to dance as the DJ played Chicago's haunting "If you leave me now" and put both his arms around her as they swayed together in the darkened room, lit only by the slow red, yellow and blue blinks of the lights. She had drunk enough to be carelessly relaxed and was only half aware that he did not change the way he was holding her or how they were dancing when the tempo quickened with the next record. When it finished he said he wanted to show her something and took her hand as she followed him out of the room. She smiled at Norman who was still in the hall talking to the man about Regency glass and wondered why he looked back at her so resentfully.

Dunford led her out of the house again and down the night-covered garden, the sounds of the party fading behind them, until they reached the private stillness beyond the trellis, its honeysuckle silence amplified by the muffled music and voices from the house. Tess warily marshalled her defences to deal with the pass she felt was inevitably coming.

"You were asking me about my family last night," Dunford said unexpectedly. He indicated a wooden door in the end wall of the garden. "We can get through to the church this way. I'll show you the Pembury mausoleum."

"Surely they keep the church locked at night?"

"I've got the key for our private chapel," he replied, opening the door. "I promise you it's fascinating."

Tess, who had stopped several paces behind him, reflected that being chased round a tomb by a randy aristocrat who conveniently brought the chapel key to a party would certainly be fascinating. But it had all been so charmingly done that she could not imagine him turning unpleasant; if he did, she knew several ways of bringing tears to his eyes. She stepped through the door as Dunford held it open for her and they walked towards the moon-grey church, looming up against the stars in front of them.

Observing the high proportion of guests whose adolescence would have begun in the age of wide skirts, shoestring ties and milk bars, the DJ lined up a series of records which would trigger their memories and make them temporarily forget the physical limitations of creeping middle age. For thirty minutes the room was filled with the formative rocking beat of their generation. Presley's "Jailhouse Rock"; Chubby Checker twisting again; Jerry Lee Lewis; Bill Haley; The Ramones; the Stones' "Satisfaction" and "Brown Sugar"; the "Good Vibrations" of the Beach Boys; the Beatles' raw "Twist and Shout" and joyous "I wanna hold your hand". As the DJ let them down with McCartney's wistful "Yesterday" and Simon and Garfunkel's "Bridge over Troubled Water", the dancers collapsed against each other, breathless, laughing and exhilarated. It would be worth the aching backs and stiffened joints of the morning to have danced again with the years of Espresso coffee, Mary Quant and the glittering, betrayed Camelot of living Kennedys.

Maltravers had finally got rid of the woman whose "little modest writing" had turned out to be poetry of the greetings card and pokerwork school, without actually committing himself to promising an opinion on her dire rhyming couplets. Peter and Susan had left and he wondered where Tess was. He could not see her anywhere on the ground floor of the house but realised that the party had spread itself to the first-floor living rooms as well and went up the wide stairs from one corner of the hall to the balcony landing above to explore. The last room he reached was Trevor Darby's study, which was also used for

61

cricket club committee meetings. Two men were settling an argument about record fourth-wicket stands in Test matches between England and the West Indies from the almost complete collection of *Wisden Cricketers' Almanack* that filled one bookcase; the accumulation of recondite statistics was among the many aspects of the game that Tess found meaningless. Standing apart from them, Luke Norman was looking out of the window.

"Hello again," said Maltravers as he joined him. "You haven't seen Tess anywhere about, have you?"

"Miss Davy? No. I think she's with Simon."

There was unmistakable annoyance in Norman's reply. The two men left the room to celebrate the settling of their argument with another drink.

"If you find them you might tell Simon I'm up here and would like to talk to him," Norman added, still gazing through the window at the nearby houses on the opposite side of Bellringer Street. Maltravers found it interesting that he was clearly not prepared to go and look for Dunford himself. It seemed childish, a condition possibly brought on by too many glasses of wine; Norman was speaking with artificial precision as though not confident that he had complete control of his tongue.

"Of course," Maltravers said. "I don't imagine they've run off together."

The look of fury Norman flashed towards him at this immaterial piece of banter, before turning away again, was vivid. Maltravers left the room, reflecting that certain suppositions he had made earlier appeared to be correct. He noticed another set of stairs near the study door, presumably used by the servants in an earlier age of the house, and went down them to find they led to the kitchen, its table covered with still substantial reserves of wine in bottles and boxes and the room filled with another swarm of guests. As he refilled his glass someone spoke to him and he was drawn into the talk again.

"The BBC? It's nothing more than an annexe of the Kremlin" . . .
*"He knows as much about the menopause as I do about his blasted
Masons"* . . . *"Don't talk to me about people offering to lay a
garden path"* . . . *"Been living with the chap for two years and now
she wants me to pay for a white wedding."*

Tess's laughter rippled through the high, still silence of St
Barbara's, echoing off walls pierced with tall, narrow windows
of muted stained glass which let in the only gloomy illumina-
tion. The sound came from the Pembury chapel on the south
side of the altar, ringing across dark oak pews and fading into
shadows of Saxon and Norman stone.

"Simon, you're joking!" she protested.

Dunford grinned as he shook his head in denial.

"I promise you I'm not," he insisted. "Hubert, the fifth Earl,
was absolutely barmy. He was convinced he could fly, leapt off
the roof of Edenbridge House to prove it and landed right on
top of his mother-in-law who was visiting them. She was killed
– after all, she was nearly ninety – but he survived, dashed back
upstairs and tried it again. This time he killed the butler who
had gone to help her. The family had the devil of a job keeping it
quiet."

Tess shook her head disbelievingly. "You're making it up."

"Believe me, it's all in the family papers. Even the bribes they
had to pay to various people to keep it hushed up. Look at this."

He led her to where a small plaque was set in the wall and
pointed to the inscription as he read it aloud.

"'Obediah Bottomley, 1740 – 1813. Died in the service of the
family'. Now how does a family retainer, however faithful, end
up in the family vault? Only because the sixth Earl felt so guilty
about his death that he wanted to make the gesture. The story's
not in the guidebooks – for obvious reasons we'd rather keep
quiet about insanity in the family – but I assure you it's
absolutely true."

"Then if you'd prefer to keep it quiet, why are you telling

me?" Tess's voice added several layers of interrogation to the question.

"Oh, it's not all that secret," Dunford replied indifferently. "It's a curiosity I like to share with certain people."

Tess wondered how certain people were selected – and how many other available women had been entertained with the incredible story on the same private tour.

"And are any more of you mad?" she asked casually.

"Not in the conventional sense. A few eccentrics here and there, but otherwise quite normal." Dunford paused and looked at her quizzically. "There are no hereditary problems or anything like that, I'm happy to say."

It was, Tess felt, a much more subtle line than the one used by a television producer at a first-night party when he had explained how successful his vasectomy had been. And it was, at last, something that could be recognised as a line. For the previous half-hour she had felt as safe as if she had been with her own brother, which was not what she had been anticipating. She was puzzled and mildly disappointed; it would have been interesting to see how one of the most eligible bachelors on the matrimonial hit lists of several titled families operated. Now, perhaps . . . but Dunford had turned away from her, almost as if he was uncomfortable about the implications of his remark.

"We ought to be getting back," he said. "I've monopolised you much too long."

As they returned through the silent and darkened church-yard, the faint clamour of the party growing louder as they approached the gate in the garden wall, Tess could make no sense of their private excursion. Dunford had blatantly flirted with her while they danced and had deliberately taken her to where they would be alone together in a setting with at least a touch of Gothic romance. He had been attentive, amusing and flattering and then – she smiled to herself as the parallel struck her – he really had just shown her his etchings. Now he seemed strangely quiet as if his mind was occupied with something. Just outside the gate he stopped by an unremarkable gravestone, obviously old and neglected, tilting like an ever-falling domino. "This is the other member of the family."

Tess glanced at him sharply. In the church he had joked about his ancestors; now he sounded immensely sad. The tombstone was half in shadow and she had to crouch down to read the worn lettering: Susannah Hawkhurst, 1835–1858. No quotation, no indication of affection, no grief of loss, just the baldest record of a name and twenty-three years of a woman's life.

"Why isn't she in the family vault?" she asked as she straightened up.

"Susannah was the youngest daughter of William, the eighth Earl," Dunford replied softly. "In Capley they borrowed the nickname of the Duke of Cumberland and called him Stinking Billy. It had been arranged that she should marry the second son of the Duke of Fennimore. There may have been a nastier man in Victorian England but I doubt it. She was in love with a captain in the eleventh Hussars. She had spirit and pleaded with her father but it was no use. She and the officer ran away together but were captured as they were boarding the Dover ferry just before it left for Calais. He was cashiered and she was brought back to Edenbridge House and confined to her room until the wedding. It sounds like a Victorian melodrama now, but such things really did happen."

Tess stiffened as an angry bitterness entered Dunford's voice.

"The night before the ceremony, they heard her screaming in her room for hours," he continued, and it was as though the tragedy had just happened. "Then she stopped. In the morning they found she had torn her wedding dress into strips and woven them into a rope and hanged herself. Only her mother's pleading allowed her to be buried in consecrated ground. Her father refused absolutely to place her in the chapel, although given the influence of the Pemburys that could probably have been arranged. For Christ's sake, they were prepared to arrange everything else in her life for her."

Dunford turned to look at Tess and the moonlight caught the anger and sorrow staining his face.

"Her mother kept the note she left and it's still in the archives. All it said was, 'I cannot do my duty'." He sighed as Tess looked at him with a questioning frown. "No, you don't understand. Very few people do. When you're born into a family like mine, duty is the iron they put in your soul. There's a terrible fear that our citadels will crumble if one of us doesn't obey. That's what killed Susannah."

Tess had to stop herself from mocking him, reminding him that it was now the late twentieth century and women had the vote. Dunford was rational and intelligent – and now tormented by something she could not understand.

"That was more than a hundred years ago," she gently reminded him.

He smiled without humour. "They have a saying in Old Capley that when you walk through the gates of Edenbridge Park you should put your watch back two hundred years. It doesn't matter how up to date we are in some ways – running the estate with computers, making videos to show to potential tourists in America – certain things simply never change. The first thing I can remember being told as a child was that one day I would be Lord Pembury. Ever since, it's been constantly hammered into me that I have no choice about it."

"Yes you have," objected Tess. "You could refuse the title. Others have."

"It's happened with a few minor titles," Dunford acknowledged. "But not in one of the really ancient families like mine. The only thing that it's like is being brought up as a devout Catholic. You can reject it as much as you want . . . but on your deathbed you beg for a priest. When my father dies, I must take the title and pass it on to my own son."

"And some people would envy you," said Tess. "A beautiful home, money, a privileged lifestyle. There are worse fates."

"Yes, I expect there are. But those who envy me don't have to

66

pay the price – and there always is a price. It's called duty and it comes before everything else." Dunford gestured towards the grave. "It killed Susannah."

A burst of sound suddenly surged over the wall as the party guests raucously joined in the chorus of the most inane pop song. Whooping, half-drunken voices were mixed with the screech of party whistles and the explosion of balloons. In another world of St Barbara's silent, grey churchyard, Tess sympathetically leaned forward and kissed Dunford's cheek. She could feel the anguish surrounding him, even though she was unable to comprehend it. But what confused her most was why he had decided to reveal something so private and painful of himself to her; she was convinced that had not been his intention when he had taken her out to the church.

Chapter Five

With her hair wound in two tight coils against her ears, Joanna York looked slightly old-fashioned, like a telephone operator left over from an old black and white film, but was at least becoming increasingly animated. Maltravers, who had found her standing on her own in one of the quieter rooms of the house, had persevered after several false starts to their conversation – she had seemed almost petrified when he had first approached her – then had chanced to ask her something about the history of Old Capley and a completely different woman had emerged. She was well-informed and as she talked, prompted by only occasional remarks from him, her confidence grew. For nearly twenty minutes he found her entertaining, even witty company, making shrewd and faintly caustic observations on various past worthies of the parish and holders of the Pembury title. Suddenly she abruptly stopped as if embarrassed.

"I'm sorry," she apologised hesitantly. "I'm . . . I talk too much sometimes."

Maltravers sensed that a lot of barriers had dropped sharply back into place and had spotted her apprehensive glance behind him just before she stopped speaking. He glanced round and saw that her husband had entered the room.

"Excuse me," she said and was gone. Maltravers watched her walk straight over to York as if his very appearance had been an unspoken summons and raised his eyebrows disparagingly. He found such submissive behaviour unhealthy, particularly in a woman who clearly had a personality of her own, however stultified it may have become.

The party had changed into its after-midnight gear; about half the guests had left and the ones that remained were slowing down. Maltravers strolled out to the door leading into the garden as Tess and Dunford walked back towards the house.

"We were just about to send search parties," he remarked.

"Sorry. I've been showing Tess the family vault," said Dunford. "I couldn't see you around anywhere or you could have come with us. I hope you don't mind."

Tess's eyes flickered warningly, cutting off any comment Maltravers might have made.

"Not in the least," he replied equably. "However, Luke's been wondering where you'd got to. He was upstairs in the study when I last saw him. Said he wanted to talk to you about something."

Dunford looked uneasy. "I expect I'd better go and see what he wants . . . You're not leaving yet, are you?"

"Not for a while. It's a very good party . . . and I want to dance with Tess."

"I'll see you shortly then." As Dunford walked past them towards the hall, Maltravers looked at Tess closely as she watched him go.

"Another drink?" he suggested mildly. "There still appear to be copious gallons left."

She nodded absently. "Yes, please . . . That was all very strange." She turned and smiled at him. "I'm sorry, darling, I didn't realise how long we'd been gone. You weren't worried, were you?"

"In the circumstances, there was hardly anything for me to worry about, was there?" Maltravers raised his eyebrows, blandly interrogative.

"What do you mean by that?"

Maltravers looked surprised that she did not understand him. "Don't be obtuse, darling. You were perfectly safe with Simon. Surely you knew that?"

69

It still took her several seconds to realise what he meant then she closed her eyes and tapped her fingers against her forehead as though trying to send a message through to her brain.

"Of course!" She shook her head, reprimanding herself for her lack of perception. "You stupid cow! When did you know?"

"It crossed my mind when they arrived together," said Maltravers. "When I spoke to Luke a short while ago I was certain."

"Then . . ." Tess frowned as she reassessed what had happened in the church. "Then what was all that about? I thought he was going to make a pass at me and at one moment he almost did. What was he playing at?"

"I don't know, but if you want an educated guess, I think it may be crunch time for Simon," said Maltravers. "Whatever his personal inclinations are in matters sexual, he's going to have to change his ways fairly soon. The time is rapidly approaching when he's going to have to marry and produce an heir. He doesn't really – "

" – have any choice," Tess interrupted, finally understanding a great many things. "And *that's* what he meant about Susannah. I cannot do my duty."

"Susannah? Who's she?" Maltravers looked mystified.

"Get me that drink and I'll tell you all about it. Our little trip to the family vault suddenly becomes very interesting indeed."

Having failed to make any progress in his conversation with York, Oliver Hawkhurst had indulged in his customary habit of seeing what sexual action might be available at the party. A woman whose husband had walked out on her after ten years of marriage was offering distinct possibilities. She was over-eagerly interested in any man who paid her any attention and was not greatly particular over who she found to occupy the empty desert of her double bed. Hawkhurst was finding it almost embarrassing for matters to be so easy as Dunford walked past them in the hall and went upstairs.

"Actually I never stopped taking the Pill," the woman remarked casually, looking at Hawkhurst archly. "After all . . . well, you never know, do you?"

"No, you don't."

After that it was only a matter of establishing which front door in Bellringer Street would be on the latch when he discreetly left a short while after she did. His wife and three children were as irrelevant to her as they were to him. Only their motives differed: in her case, a matter of eating when you happen to be hungry, in his the common practice among certain husbands who buttress flimsy egos by deluding themselves that women – preferably younger women – sleep with them because they are irresistible. The woman gave him a lascivious look of promise as she went out of the front door. He was the third prospect she had tried that evening and his smug self satisfaction would have been fatally undermined had he known that she regarded him as only a marginally better alternative than another night spent alone with Edna O'Brien and a very large gin.

Dunford hesitated outside the closed door of the study, trying to wade through the emotions that were washing about him. The interlude with Tess in the church had compounded his confusion and the inevitable image of Susan Penrose that came into his mind only made the whole thing a bigger and more tormenting mess. Luke's refusal to accept the situation by simply turning up at Edenbridge House again had thrown him off balance just as he had thought he was beginning to sort himself out. There were too many pressures, too many complications and Dunford was rocking helplessly between what he wanted to do and what he knew he would be forced to do.

As he pushed the door open, Norman was sitting at Trevor Darby's desk holding one of a pair of cricket balls, commemorating some distant and forgotten victories, that rested on

71

small plinths in front of him. He glanced up cynically as Dunford entered then returned his attention to the battered blood-red sphere in his hands.

"And was the lovely Miss Davy satisfactory?" he asked. "You always did swing both ways, didn't you darling?"

Dunford closed the door behind him. "Nothing has happened with Miss Davy."

Norman tossed the ball a few inches into the air and caught it again.

"Wouldn't she play? Or couldn't she turn you on?"

"If you're just going to be crude, Luke, there's no point in talking to you. If you think I owe you an apology, then I'm sorry that I used Tess to try and make a point to you. You're going to have to accept that it's got to finish between us. I've told you enough times that I don't have any choice about getting married."

Norman looked at him bitterly for a moment then stood up and crossed the space between them.

"Which is exactly what you told Harry, isn't it?" he demanded. Dunford looked away uncomfortably. "Oh yes, he told me all about that. He said he believed you until you turned up with me three weeks later. And how long did it last with him? Two years? It's our second anniversary next month."

He was standing so close that Dunford could smell the whisky on his breath as he moved past him and went over to the window.

"All right, it was just an excuse for Harry, but it's the truth for you." He spoke with his back to Norman. "My father has tolerated my behaviour up to now but he has made it quite clear that it's got to stop. If I were to die without producing an heir everything would go to Oliver – and that happens to matter a lot."

He turned to face Norman, urgently pleading.

"For Christ's sake, Luke, can't you see the position I'm in? I don't have complete freedom about what I do with my life. I've even been told who I'm expected to marry. There are only three choices and two of them I can't stand. It would be exactly the same if I'd spent the last ten years screwing every woman I could find. At the end of it I'd have to ditch them for a wife."

"Balls, Simon," snapped Norman. "Your father was over forty before he married, you're just using this as an excuse. You could play the gay scene for years and that's exactly what you're going to do. I know all about that Guards officer while I was away in Hanover. Is he the one you've got lined up to take my place?"

"Listen!" Dunford was suddenly angry with exasperation. "I've spent the last year trying to come to terms with this. As you so charmingly put it, I swing both ways and I happen to find both satisfactory – it hasn't just been men in the past year. I've sorted out what I want, now get off my back!"

"*What you want?*" Norman shouted. "You bloody, titled bastard! Do you think this is still the Middle Ages when the Lord of the Manor can have it off with any peasant he fancies? How many of us are there? Ten? Twenty?"

As Norman screamed at Dunford, there were suddenly three men in the house who wanted to kill him, one for greed, one for vengeance and one for love.

Half-lit by the flickering disco lights coming through the open French doors, Maltravers and Tess sat on the low wall by the steps of the terrace in the warm darkness. The figures in the room were silhouettes, the arabesques of their lazy movements picked up in a slow kaleidoscope of shadows appearing and vanishing on the walls. Peggy Lee sang the sentimental story of the folk who lived on the hill. The party was fading away like a glowing fire.

"So what do you think?" Maltravers asked when Tess had finished recounting her confusing visit to St Barbara's and the tombs of the Pemburys with Dunford.

"That he is very unhappy, that he's probably still in love with Luke Norman but knows it's hopeless. The way that Luke looked at me when Simon and I went out of the house together means he's angry about it. And . . ." Tess screwed up her lips as if trying to unravel something. "And I can only assume that Simon started out meaning to make a pass at me to . . . I don't know. Prove something to himself?"

"That's possible. But you say he didn't."

"No . . . but I'm sure he *wanted* to. There was something in his face in the chapel when he looked at me, as though . . ." She shook her head in her own confusion.

"As though his life would be so much easier if he wasn't Lord Dunford – and all that means – and wasn't gay," said Maltravers. "It's perfectly obvious why he identifies with the unhappy Susannah."

Tess glanced at Maltravers inquiringly. "Why does he *have* to get married? For God's sake, Edenbridge House will survive if he doesn't. It's been there long enough."

"That's not the point," he replied. "Edenbridge represents something, it's part of a dynastic process. We are dealing with the ancient aristocracy who do not operate by our standards. Lord Pembury cannot understand my sense of values any more than I can understand his. I can't imagine what it's really like to have the responsibility of owning Edenbridge House or how important it would be that my son should inherit it. But I can imagine that it might matter a great deal."

"But if Simon doesn't have children for any reason, it will still stay in the family. Didn't you say his cousin is next in line?"

"Yes, but Lord Pembury may not relish the prospect. Simon has been brought up to be Lord Pembury and run Edenbridge in a certain way. Cousin Oliver apparently wants to turn it into a funfair. When you've got pictures on the walls of ancestors who could have known Pepys, you have a special perspective of such things. And when you die you leave a great deal more than a suburban semi-detached and a few life insurance policies. You're caught up in an historical process."

He finished his drink and stood up.

"Anyway, if we can't understand it, there's little point in speculating about it. It would seem that Simon is now having to select the next Lady Dunford – which is certainly not likely to be you, my love – and Luke Norman is not best pleased. A fascinating glimpse into the lifestyle of the very upper classes, but nothing to do with us. A last dance and we go?"

They left their glasses on the wall and stepped into the lounge, two more shadows in the gloom now wrapped in Nat King Cole's timeless "Unforgettable". The clockwork spring of the party had almost completely unwound from its earlier frantic tension. Apart from the dancers, a group of guests in the kitchen were examining the remaining bottles, a couple on the stairs were earnestly discussing God, a young man had passed out in the lavatory and Joanna York was refusing to dance with a member of the Estate cricket team as she waited for her husband to reappear. As Luke Norman slipped out of the front door without saying goodnight to anyone, Trevor and Evelyn Darby were telling each other it had been a wonderful farewell party. On the floor of the study, Dunford's dead and sightless eyes were fixed on the ceiling as blood surged from a massive, battered cavity in his head and soaked into the carpet, darkening from vivid scarlet to black.

Nat King Cole faded away and a very young Sinatra announced that it was a lovely way to spend an evening.

Alister York found that he could think surprisingly clearly as he looked down at the body. He had certainly not planned it this way, but his mind was able to grasp the situation then race through what would follow, identifying the obvious problems. He even smiled as a particularly clever touch occurred to him, then he unhesitatingly knelt down. It took less than a minute to accomplish what he wanted to do then he paused only briefly to make sure he had made no mistakes before hurrying out of the room and down the back stairs to the kitchen where Trevor and Evelyn Darby were saying goodnight to Maltravers and Tess.

"Trevor!"

Darby turned, startled by the sharp urgency in York's voice. "What's the matter?"

"Can you come upstairs please? Now."

"Hang on a minute, Alister. The place isn't on fire, is it?"

York strode across the kitchen, his agitation slicing through the air of tired inertia as people stared at him.

"Come upstairs," he repeated. "Lord Dunford's been murdered. In your study."

Standing nearby, Joanna York dropped her glass, its shattering tinkle mingling with her muted scream; only her husband noticed. Darby stared at him as if he had cracked a distasteful joke.

"Alister, are you drunk?" he demanded.

"Just come with me," York replied grimly, stepping to one side and implicitly inviting Darby to go up first. Darby hesitated for a moment, looking at York's face closely, then crossed towards the door leading to the stairs.

"Just wait here, dear," he called back to his wife. "I'll sort this out." He gave the clear impression that he simply did not believe what York had told him.

"I'm going too," Maltravers murmured as the two men went out of the kitchen. "See if you can find Luke Norman anywhere."

"What for?" Tess asked.

"I sent Simon up to the study because Luke wanted to talk to him. Just see if he's around."

As Maltravers entered the study, York and Darby were standing on the far side of the desk staring at the floor. Darby knelt down and was feeling in vain for a pulse in Dunford's wrist as Maltravers crossed the room and saw for himself. As he took in the shock and ugliness of the crushed head, he was struck by the suggestion that there was something about the body that was wrong, something . . . he was still trying to identify it as Darby stood up.

"He's dead. Good God." He shook his head in disbelief. "I'll call the police . . . I'm sorry I didn't believe you, Alister. How long ago did you find him?"

"Only a few minutes. I came straight down to tell you."

"And how did you happen to find him?" Maltravers asked quietly and saw the spurt of anger cross York's face before he replied.

"My wife and I were about to leave and I was looking for him to say goodnight," he replied curtly, making it clear he did not think it was Maltravers' place to question him. "I couldn't see him downstairs so I came up here because I knew people had been using this room during the evening."

York drew in his breath and looked straight at Maltravers, challenging him to probe further.

"That doesn't matter at the moment," Darby interposed. "I'll lock this room and call the police from the phone downstairs."

"And we'd better make sure nobody else leaves the house," York added. "I don't think this happened very long ago."

Maltravers and Darby looked back at the body where the still-throbbing blood emphasised York's comment – and this time Maltravers grasped what did not make sense.

"Where's his tie?" he asked.

"Was he wearing one?" Darby said.

"Oh, yes. It was his Vincent's tie. I commented upon it earlier."

Darby shrugged. "He probably took it off because it was warm."

"And left his top shirt button fastened?" Maltravers objected. "That hardly makes sense. Is there any sign of it anywhere?"

As all three men turned and looked round the study, the front door opened downstairs and Oliver Hawkhurst slipped away into the night.

"Just a minute!" exclaimed Darby. "The ball's gone! That must be what . . . They've both gone!"

77

He gestured towards the top of the desk where both the plinths for the pair of cricket balls now stood empty.

"Trevor, we're not here to play detectives," York said impatiently. "Call the police and I'll go and stand by the front door to make sure that nobody leaves."

"What about the garden?" Maltravers asked. "I understand there's a way out into the churchyard . . . It's all right, leave that with me."

The immediate oddities of Dunford's murder rattled about Maltravers' mind as he dashed downstairs, grabbed Tess and took her out with him into the garden to stand at the top of the terrace steps where they could see anyone who left through the back of the house.

"Any sign of Luke Norman?" he asked urgently.

"Not that I can see. Unless he's upstairs."

"Possibly, but I don't think so. And if he's left the house then I think he's going to have some explaining to do. He was in the study when I spoke to him before you and Simon came back from the church . . . What time is it? Nearly twenty past one . . . so it must have been under an hour ago. When you came back, I told Simon he was there and wanted to talk to him. Now he's vanished. It looks very persuasive."

"Then Simon really is dead?" As Maltravers turned to Tess he could see sudden shock and grief gathering in her eyes.

"Yes, I'm afraid he is," he said gently, putting his arm around her and drawing her close to him comfortingly. "I'm sorry. I liked him as well."

"How was he killed?"

"He was hit very hard on the head, apparently with a cricket ball. The odd thing is that two of them appear to be missing which doesn't make much sense . . . and there's something else that's curious as well." He explained about the Vincent's tie.

"He certainly had it on when I was with him," said Tess. "Why should he have taken it off?"

78

"You're assuming that he did. Supposing the murderer removed it?"

"What on earth for?"

Maltravers lit a cigarette, expelling the smoke slowly and thoughtfully. "A souvenir of an old affair? These foolish things remind me of you and all that."

Tess shuddered. "That's sick! Would Luke Norman do something like that? Would anybody?"

"We don't know what Luke Norman was like, we only met him this evening and hardly spoke to him," said Maltravers. "But if he was jealous or possessive enough to murder Simon so that nobody else could have him, let's not start looking for rational behaviour anywhere else. From what we know, it doesn't take much imagination to suppose that Luke Norman had a motive for killing Simon and he certainly had the opportunity. Now he's vanished. All circumstantial, but very heavy indeed. The business of the tie makes a perverted sort of sense if that's the case."

"And I suppose we have to tell the police all this?" Tess appeared hesitant.

"Too right," said Maltravers firmly. "This is no time for woolly liberal ideas about forgiving crimes of passion or not making accusations without proof. Simon was a nice man and I want to see whoever it was nailed for his murder. I'm not saying it was Luke Norman, but it looks very much that way."

Distantly, from the direction of the New Town, they heard the two-note blare of a police siren, dramatic but unnecessary on empty night roads, fading and growing again as it weaved into Old Capley and howled up Bellringer Street before dying away; like Chesterton's wood, the garden was suddenly full of two policemen. Trevor and Evelyn Darby's final party had ended and something hideous had begun. As the police rounded up the guests – including the befuddled young man in the lavatory who had slept though the commotion – and herded them together in one room, Maltravers noticed there was no sign of Luke Norman. As they all waited uncomfortably, trying to catch what the police were saying out in the hall, it also occurred to him that he could not see Oliver Hawkhurst either.

The police realised very quickly that the situation facing them was both delicate and complex. Delicate because, while Death ticks off the names of down-and-outs and millionaires with equal indifference, the body of an aristocrat with his head murderously smashed in is not the same thing as a dipsomaniac tramp found stiff in a ditch. Complex because there were twenty-seven people in the same house as the corpse. Statements had to be taken from them all as the scene-of-crimes officer began his meticulous examination, collecting the fragments of possible evidence – many probably irrelevant – which could form the underpinning of an arrest and charge. As photographs were taken, adhesive tape pressed on the study carpet to collect dust, fingerprints searched for and all the minutiae collected, the guests were asked what they could remember about an evening during which they had had no reason to notice what was going on. Unless they were offered an emotional confession on a plate, the police were concentrating on the two natural questions: opportunity and motive. The first was impossible. Guest after guest could only give the vaguest indication of their movements at any time of the evening and it rapidly became clear that virtually any one of them could have slipped upstairs and committed almost any number of murders. But investigation into motive was more interesting – and pointed in two different directions.

People were summoned one at a time into the two rooms the police had taken over for questioning the guests as more officers arrived at the house. As Maltravers was led through to the sitting room, he saw a man who he supposed was the doctor being let in the front door and taken upstairs. He gave his name and address and a brief account of his own movements during the party as far as he could recall them over more than four hours.

"There is something else I want to tell you," he added. "Although I must stress that I have no proof whatever that it may be significant. I am pretty certain that Lord Dunford may have been having a homosexual affair with a man called Luke Norman who was here earlier. I also think that Lord Dunford wished to end the relationship and Mr Norman was angry about it. I spoke to Mr Norman in the study sometime after midnight and he asked me to send Lord Dunford up there. About an hour later, when I saw Lord Dunford again, I told him."

Detective Sergeant David Parry, one of the first CID officers to arrive at the house, looked at him thoughtfully.

"And do you know where Mr Norman is now?" he asked.

"No – and I have not seen him here since Lord Dunford's body was discovered. As far as I know, he is staying at Edenbridge House for the weekend and I rather think you will find that he drives a white MG."

Parry excused himself and left the room, giving Maltravers time to consider the implications of what he had said. It was an uncomfortable feeling to have suggested that a man he did not know – to all intents, a complete stranger – could be a murderer, but he could not see that he had any alternative. Luke Norman was the last person Maltravers had seen in the study; Dunford had been killed there; Maltravers strongly suspected that Luke Norman had motive and now he had disappeared. If Norman turned out to be innocent, Maltravers would feel guilty about this suggestion, but if he said nothing and Norman got away with it he would feel worse. It was not a happy position to be in. Parry, who had sent two officers to Edenbridge House to see if they could find Luke Norman, returned.

"I appreciate that what you have told me is supposition on your part," he said. "However, I would like you to repeat it for an official statement. I would also like to know how well you personally knew Lord Dunford and Mr Norman."

"Hardly at all. I met Lord Dunford for the first time last night after the concert at Edenbridge House, although I knew of him from his cricketing career, of course. We played together in the cricket match between the Estate and Town teams and I spoke to him at the party – which is where I met Mr Norman for the first time." Maltravers smiled comprehendingly. "I take the point of your question, Sergeant, but I'm not a very likely suspect, am I?"

"We have to keep an open mind, sir," Parry replied flatly. "However, as long as you tell us where we can contact you again if necessary, I don't think we need detain you after you have given your statement and been searched."

"May I wait until you've finished with Miss Davy?"

"Yes – unless we have reason to detain her of course."

"I don't think you will, although she may be able to add to what I have told you. We're both staying with Mr and Mrs Penrose across the road at number ten for the next few days. If this matter isn't cleared up by the time we leave, I'll let you know where you can contact us."

Maltravers gave his statement, then was taken out into the hall where a policeman carried out a north-to-south search of him, an elementary operation in the hunt for the murder weapon being taken with all the guests before they were allowed to leave. He was told he could wait for Tess in the hall, and as he sat beneath a signed photograph of Bradman he saw Alister York being taken through to give his statement. After a few minutes, Parry reappeared out of the interview room and spoke to an officer standing near Maltravers, who just overheard the name of Oliver Hawkhurst before the policeman left the house. Craning his neck as discreetly as he could, Maltravers looked through the window on his left and saw him using the radio in one of the police cars parked outside. Back in the interview room, York was enlarging on what he had said.

"You will almost certainly discover this for yourselves in any event. The simple fact is that Mr Hawkhurst is in considerable financial difficulties over which Lord Pembury – and I believe

Lord Dunford – had refused to assist him. With Lord Dunford's death Mr Hawkhurst becomes the heir to the title, Edenbridge House and everything that goes with it."

"And Mr Hawkhurst was at the party?" Parry confirmed.

"He was. He spoke to me – and that conversation, incidentally, was connected with his financial problems and the possibility of Lord Pembury helping him – then I noticed him talking to a woman in the hall sometime after midnight. I do not know when he left the house."

"Who was the woman?" Parry asked.

"A Mrs Harper . . . I think her first name is Harriet. She lives somewhere towards the bottom of Bellringer Street but I'm not certain which number."

"Mrs . . . Harper," Parry repeated as he swiftly read through the list of the guests the police had found in the house. The name was not on it. "And when was Mr Hawkhurst due to leave Edenbridge?"

"As far as I know, on Monday morning."

"Thank you, Mr York. Another officer will take your statement."

Parry left the room and radioed CID headquarters from his car with a message for Chief Superintendent Keith Miller who would be in charge of the inquiry.

"Inform Mr Miller that there are two possible leading suspects, neither of whom are in the house," he said. "Efforts are being made to locate them."

Neither the Vincent's tie, nor either one of the missing cricket balls, nor anything else that might have been used as a weapon emerged as the guests were searched; and when Parry learned that neither Norman nor Hawkhurst had returned to Edenbridge, the process of people being allowed to leave speeded up. With uncomfortable words of sympathy for their shattered host and hostess, the guests hurried away, anxious to escape the stunned atmosphere. Apart from the first police siren, the murder had caused little disturbance in Bellringer

Street which remained silent as dawn seeped into the eastern sky. As Maltravers and Tess crossed the road to the Penroses, the song of an early blackbird bubbled through the early-morning quietness from a tree in the churchyard. They let themselves in by the kitchen door and Tess started to make a cup of tea.

"I don't feel like bed," she said. "And anyway, we'd better stay up and tell Peter and Susan what's happened. When did they leave?"

"While you and Simon were at the church," said Maltravers. "Sometime after eleven I think. Pity we didn't go earlier as well, it would have saved a lot of hassle."

"Well, at least we were able to put the police in the picture about Luke Norman," said Tess, peering into a collection of tins on the work surface to discover where Susan kept the tea bags.

"Yes, but are we right? Somebody else – and I'm fairly positive it's Alister York – may have brought cousin Oliver into the picture. Remember him at the match?"

Tess, who had just had one surprise when she discovered that tea-bags lived in a tin marked mustard, turned to him inquiringly.

"It was only something I half overheard," Maltravers explained. "But that chap Parry appeared to be giving instructions to find Oliver. And that ties in with something Simon told me: on his death, Oliver is next in line."

"Are we wrong about Luke then?"

"Possibly. After all, we could only tell the police what we knew which, on the face of it, seems highly persuasive. But there was no sign of cousin Oliver anywhere about the place after Simon's body was discovered and – "

"Yes there was," Tess interrupted. "I saw him when I was looking for Luke Norman after you went upstairs. He was just going out of the front door."

"Was he, by God? Well, well, well." Maltravers rocked back on the kitchen chair and gazed at the ceiling. "He actually left the house just after Alister York said he had found the body."

84

"Yes, but he might not have known about it," Tess objected. "We only knew because we happened to be in the kitchen with Trevor and Evelyn when York came down. The word was beginning to spread but not that fast."

"Nonetheless, Simon had not been dead for very long when York found him – I know that from seeing the body myself – so it is quite possible that Oliver did it. York didn't say to Trevor or me that he had seen anybody near the study . . . but perhaps he told the police that he saw Oliver. Interesting."

Tess squeezed the tea bags against the sides of the mugs with a spoon, deep in new thoughts.

"If it was Luke, he did it for love . . . or jealousy," she said. "If it was Oliver he did it for money."

"Classic motives all round," observed Maltravers.

"Unless there's somebody else of course."

"Three potential murderers in one house? Don't you think that's overkill? Sorry, I wasn't trying to be funny."

For the next hour they sat in the kitchen discussing the murder and trying to conjure up theories about the stolen tie and why both cricket balls should have disappeared. Outside, from across the road, they heard the occasional sound of the Darbys' front door opening and closing and faint footsteps as people made their way down Bellringer Street. Beneath the limp calm of the morning the shockwaves of bloody murder were spreading with uncanny softness, a trickle of snow accumulating relentlessly towards an avalanche. Old Capley did not know the horror it would wake up to. It was seven o'clock when the silence of the house was distantly pierced by the brisk cheeping of an alarm clock, cut off after only a few seconds, before there was the sound of movement from the bedroom above their heads. Maltravers and Tess looked at each other uneasily as footsteps descended the stairs and Peter appeared in the doorway.

"God, are you still up?" he said in sleepy surprise. "Is the party still going on?"

"The party finished some hours ago," Maltravers told him. "I'm afraid we've got some bad news."

Peter, who had been shuffling instinctively towards the electric kettle, stopped and looked at him sharply.

"What's the matter? You're both all right, aren't you?"

"We're fine," Maltravers assured him. "But I'm afraid that Simon is dead. He's been murdered."

Peter stared at him for several seconds as though waiting for him to say something else then looked suddenly depressed. "Jesus, you're not joking, are you?"

"I wish I was. Sit down and we'll tell you about it."

Peter listened in silence while Tess made more tea and Maltravers quietly recounted the events of the previous few hours.

"Thank you," he said distantly, as Tess placed a mug in front of him.

"I've made one for Susan," Tess said gently. "I think you'd better go up and tell her."

Peter shook his head as if to dispel some sort of trance.

"Pardon? Oh, yes, I'll . . . Christ Almighty!" It had all sunk in, but he appeared unable to comprehend it as he stared into space in disbelief. "I'll be back down in . . ."

He left the kitchen looking as though he was trying to find some explanation that would make it all go away. After a few moments Tess and Maltravers winced as they heard Susan's cry from upstairs and a few minutes later she came down, Peter protectively holding her arm. Tears were running down her shock-crinkled features.

"Come and sit down," Tess said firmly and led her like a child to a chair. Susan's reaction was different from her husband's; where Peter had been numbed, she appeared gripped by some sort of panic, eyes gazing wildy and trembling violently. After a few seconds she looked round at them all as though seeing them for the first time, half pleading, half desperate.

"Don't you think you'd better go back to bed?" Tess suggested. "We'll take care of the children's breakfast."

"No . . . no." Susan spoke like an automaton. "I'll do that . . . I'll have to . . . I must . . ." She started to stand up, one hand pressing against the immense swelling at the front of her nightdress.

"Darling, the baby . . ." Peter began, stepping towards her. The words had an eruptive effect. Susan gave a scream of anguish, slapping her hand over her mouth to stop it as she backed away from him. Peter moved swiftly to her side and tried to put his arm round her shoulders but she shook him off savagely.

"Don't touch me! Go away!"

"Come on," he said soothingly. "Let's get you upstairs and – "

"*Let me go!*"

Her reaction was now so violent that for a moment they all froze as she stared at her husband in horror, oblivious of the presence of Maltravers and Tess.

"Don't you realise?" she shouted at him. "Don't you? It's not yours! It's Simon's!"

She stared round at them all, like someone seeing the desolation of their life, then ran out of the room, faster than seemed possible in her condition. Peter suddenly pulled himself together and followed her without a word. As Tess and Maltravers stood like statues there was the sound of small footsteps and Emma appeared from her bedroom in the cellar, sleepily clutching a brown-and-yellow knitted hedgehog.

"What's the matter with Mummy?" she asked. "Why is she crying? Is the baby coming?"

Chapter Six

With the portraits of twelve generations of his ancestors as mute witnesses, Lord Pembury heard without any betrayal of emotion that his only son had been murdered from two policemen in the library of Edenbridge House at two-thirty in the morning. He thanked them for informing him, then told the butler, who had let the officers in, to see if either Hawkhurst or Norman were in their rooms. When they were not, Pembury assured the police that he would inform them immediately if either man returned to the house, and gave their home addresses. When the police had left, Pembury instructed the butler to waken his wife's personal maid and then go back to bed. The rest of the household staff could be told later in the morning. While waiting for the maid, he telephoned the senior partner of the family's solicitors at his home and asked him to come to Edenbridge House immediately. When the maid came into the library, he explained what had happened and that her mistress would need her. Then he went upstairs again and for more than an hour was alone with his wife.

Dawn had broken when he dressed and left Edenbridge House to walk out into the park and stand alone by the gate of the field in which he had watched his son ride his first horse. Overlapping images of an inquisitive, chuckling infant, coltish adolescent, hare-brained student, graceful cricketer, and be-loved young man flickered in and out of his memory like fragments of a film. Occasionally his mouth gave a bitter twitch as recollection dripped acid on raw, exposed wounds, but when he returned to the house he was completely composed and throughout the rest of that day and all the weeks that followed the grief that had ripped through him never showed itself in his public face. Protected by the same awful control, his wife personally replied to more than four hundred letters of condolence, taking as much care with those clumsily written on cheap notepaper as those postmarked from the House of Lords, several bearing Royal seals and the one signed simply Cantuar; a lifetime of learning how to do the proper thing until it was second nature held father and mother together with steel bands of correct behaviour. Those who said it was abnormal did not understand the deep-rooted English aristocracy; and none of them knew of the many nights, in the darkness and privacy of their separate rooms, when Lord and Lady Pembury wept tears of rage, disbelief and helplessness.

The atmosphere in the Penrose household was as fragile as burnt paper. Susan had angrily told Peter to leave her alone and he was sitting in the kitchen looking dazed, as Tess and Maltravers tactfully took over the demands of the children. The little boy was happily showing Maltravers his collection of machines for miniature inter-galactic warfare in plastic and Tess occupied Emma by asking her to help find things for their breakfast.

"But when is the baby coming?" the little girl asked eagerly. "I've made it a present."

"Not yet, poppet," Tess replied. "But it won't be very long. Now, where does Mummy hide the cornflakes?"

They endured an eternity of the vibrations trembling through the room, smothering them as best they could, until the mother whose turn it was to take a collection of children for their Sunday morning riding lessons arrived. She bounced into the kitchen through the side door, normality in jodhpurs and check shirt, and was mercifully discreet.

"Come on you two," she ordered briskly. "Got your riding hats? Crops? Gloves? Heads? Right, into the car. We're running late again."

As the children scampered outside, she turned to Peter.

"I've heard," she said simply. "The kids don't know? Right, I'll keep quiet about it. One of mine knows but I've warned him that if he breathes a word the pony goes straight to the glue factory. It's best they hear it from you or Susan; they were very fond of Simon. 'Bye."

Her raised voice, boisterously laying down the law to a car full of chattering children, floated in through the window, then a door slammed and the car drove away. Apprehension, drained emotions and weariness settled amid the frozen silence in the room.

"Would you like me to talk to Susan?" Tess asked quietly.

Peter looked at her gratefully. "Would you? She won't talk to me. She just told me to get out. I don't – "

"I'll take her another cup of tea," Tess interrupted. "We can't just leave her up there on her own."

Susan was back in bed, staring without seeing out of the window, when Tess opened the door. She did not look round as Tess put the teacup on the bedside table and sat down on the duvet.

"The children have gone riding," she explained.

For a moment Susan did not react, then turned and smiled thinly out of a face tarnished with tears, shiny without make-up and chestnut hair uncombed.

"Thank you . . . I'm so sorry about all this."

"Do you want to talk about it? I think you should."

"God, I've kept it bottled up inside me for so long." Susan leaned back against the pillow and sighed. "There's been nobody I could . . . do you mind?"

Tess shook her head and Susan pulled another Kleenex from the box beside her, blew her nose inelegantly, then crumpled the tissue in her fist. She looked out of the window again as she spoke.

"It was when Peter was away last year. It was half term and the children were staying with my parents. I was making some new curtains for the bathroom one evening when Simon arrived. He was upset about something and said he'd had a row with Luke Norman . . . You met him at the party didn't you? I don't know what it was about."

Tess said nothing as she filed away the implications of the remark.

"Anyway, I'd opened a bottle of wine and offered him a glass. I knew he'd had some before, but Simon never became objectionable." Susan swallowed nervously. "He stayed and we opened another bottle then he started getting maudlin. He said he needed the love of a good woman. Honestly, Tess, he was as corny as that. I knew I'd drunk too much, but I took hold of his hand and he said something about Peter being very lucky. Then he kissed me and I suddenly realised how much I liked him. Peter was away . . . and things hadn't been too good between us. I should have stopped him, but I didn't."

Her voice had gone very faint and she looked down at the shreds of the tissue which she had been absently tearing to pieces.

"I shouldn't have . . ." She began to weep, easily and guiltily. Tess took her hand and squeezed it softly.

"But you went to bed?" she coaxed. Susan gave a little bitter laugh.

"Oh, no. My conscience wouldn't let me use the bed." A trace of hysteria entered her voice. "We did it on the settee like a couple of teenagers. Christ, it was uncomfortable. Somehow it sobered us both up and he apologised and left when I told him to."

"And that was it?" Tess asked. Susan nodded. "And what happened when Peter came back?"

"Oh Tess, I made love to him like it was going out of style. I felt so bad and it wasn't his fault and I wanted him so much and . . ." She shivered slightly. "Then I found I was pregnant."

"But how long was it before Peter returned?" Tess demanded.

"A couple of days . . . and I know, I know. I've kept telling myself the baby's his because I've got to believe that it is. But the thought's always been there and it's been nearer and nearer the surface as the time's approached. I just couldn't handle it when Simon turned up after the concert, then when I heard what had happened this morning something cracked and I became convinced it really is his. I was so shocked I didn't know what I was doing or saying down there. When Peter said something about the baby, it just came out."

Tess looked at her with something like a motherly sternness. "Now let's get this straight, lady," she said. "Gus told me before we came here that you and Peter were among the happiest married couples he knows and I've seen enough in a very short time to agree with him. Good marriages can survive worse things than a casual lay that didn't even amount to a one-night stand."

"You're not married," Susan replied. "You wouldn't say that if you were."

"All right, I'm not married," Tess agreed. "But if I was, and if I really loved my husband, it would take more than a drunken tumble that didn't mean anything to make me let go. You love Peter or you wouldn't be feeling the way you do. You've been carrying this like a hair shirt for all these months. For God's sake – no, never mind God – for your sake, for Peter's, for Timmy and Emma's sake, start getting it sorted out. I know what Simon was like, hundreds of women would have fallen for that boyish charm approach. Did you talk to him about it?"

"Yes. He was dreadfully upset and said he'd stop seeing me and Peter but I told him not to be silly. We've known him ever since we moved to Old Capley and he's an old friend . . . was an old friend. I said we should just . . ." Susan gestured helplessly. Tess let go of her hand and stood up.

"I'm going downstairs to tell Peter you want to talk to him," she said firmly. "Don't argue, you're going to tell him. You owe him."

Susan's automatic protests stopped in mid-sentence.

"All right. Thank you. I just needed someone to tell me that, that was all. It will be all right, won't it?"

Tess pursed her lips. "Marriages don't come with guarantees, you have to make them work yourself. If they get broken, you can throw them away or try to mend them. I think this one is worth mending. Go for it."

As she was leaving the room, Susan called her back.

"But what about Simon? I've been so . . . I haven't been able to think about that. He's been murdered? Why? Who by?"

"Nobody knows at the moment," said Tess. "The police are sorting it out. But that's not very important to you and Peter just now."

As Tess re-entered the kitchen, Peter and Maltravers stopped talking and looked at her: Peter anxious, Maltravers inquiring.

"Susan wants to talk to you," she announced. "She wants to tell you what she's just told me."

As Peter stood up and went to walk past her, Tess took hold of his arm.

"She's very pregnant, very confused and very unhappy. Just *listen*." She watched him go, trying to assess his mood. "How is he?"

Maltravers lit his twelfth cigarette since they had returned to the house. "Disorientated is the word, I think. So what happened between Susan and Simon?"

"Not a great deal when you get down to it," said Tess. "We'd better get some sleep while they talk it out. I'll tell you upstairs. We'll leave a note and set the alarm for lunchtime."

With murder and marital mischance spinning through their minds, Maltravers and Tess fell asleep just as Oliver Hawkhurst was waking up. For a few moments he looked at the unfamiliar bedroom ceiling, grimacing through a relentless timpani drummer who had taken a lease on the inside of his head, his mouth feeling as though he had consumed vast quantities of very old blotting paper. It had been a night of over-frantic coupling, ungracious, ungainly and finally unsatisfactory; when he had flopped on to his back and started snoring within minutes of its grunting, deficient culmination, his companion had regarded him with acute distaste and decided that a repeat performance was not worth the effort involved. The anticipated pleasures of illicit passion had now left nothing more than a smell of stale sweat and a mutual realisation of the inanity of meaningless fornication, which had earlier seemed such an alluring prospect.

She remained asleep as Hawkhurst quietly slipped out of the bed and gathered up his clothes, scattered across the floor when the excitement of new flesh had been at its height; the broken threads from two lost shirt buttons were all that remained of the eager lust of the small hours of the night. He dressed hastily, feeling sticky and uncomfortable in the crumpled clothing, then showed a meaningless touch of consideration before he left. He had to think for a moment until he remembered her name, then half roused her with his hand on her naked shoulder.

"Harriet, I've got to go," he whispered. Groggy with residual alcohol and exhausted by frustrated physical effort, she made a low, irritated, growling noise at the back of her throat; the stuff of which the poets sing ended on that faint animal sound.

Hawkhurst sluiced away the worst of the roasted salt permeating his mouth with a glass of water from the sink in the back kitchen, noticing there was a door leading out into the small, paved, courtyard garden behind the house, which offered a more discreet exit than skulking out of the front. The garden, like the Darbys' higher up the street, also had a door in the end wall, but this time leading on to a narrow, stony alleyway running behind several houses. He followed it up the hill and found his way into a corner of the churchyard and through there to another way out by the Bellringer Street lodge. A few people arriving for morning service took no notice as he passed near them and walked on into Edenbridge Park. He had decided that his appearance, crumpled, unwashed and un-shaven, would only lead to difficult questions at the house and he made his way round to the private car park, intending simply to drive home and telephone with some sort of explanation later.

As he crunched across the gravel he stiffened as he saw two uniformed policemen standing next to his car. He thought about turning away, but they had already seen him approaching, keys visible in his hand. All he could do was pretend to ignore them as if their presence could have nothing to do with him; it required a considerable effort.

"Mr Oliver Hawkhurst?" one of them asked as he reached the car.

"Yes. What do you want?" He made his voice sound brusque and impatient, a gentleman not accustomed to being accosted by the police.

"We are officers with Capley police, Sir, and would like you to accompany us to the station."

Hawkhurst looked the constable up and down coldly, the mask of his face covering panic-riddled thoughts; there was more than one matter in his life in which he would rather the police did not take too close an interest.

"What the devil for?" he demanded, with as much cocksure arrogance as he could gather together.

"Your cousin, Lord Dunford, has been found murdered, sir, and we have reason to believe that you may be able to assist with police inquiries into this matter."

Both policemen later reported that Oliver Hawkhurst went very white at that moment.

Maltravers and Tess entered the kitchen again cautiously to find their friends going through the motions of living their lives.

"Oh, why didn't you stay in bed?" Susan was sorting out the contents of the kitchen rubbish drawer as though the tedious occupation was very important to her. "You must be worn out."

"We're all right," Maltravers assured her. "We can catch up on some sleep tonight."

"Then are you hungry? I'm sorry, I haven't thought about lunch."

"Don't bother for us," Tess said. "We're going down to the pub to grab something."

"Are you sure? It's no trouble . . . I'll have to . . ." Susan looked at them hesitantly. "We thought you might not want to stay now."

"Would you like us to?" asked Maltravers.

Susan looked at Peter, who was filling in the o's in the headlines of the *Sunday Times*.

"If you don't mind," she said. "We . . . think it might help. But . . ."

"Then we stay," said Maltravers firmly. "Apart from anything else, an abrupt departure might give the police the wrong impression at the moment. I told them we were staying here for a few days and if they find we've gone they might jump to all sorts of conclusions. Of course, you don't know the full story yet do you?"

"We know." Peter threw down his pen, suddenly provoked by the meaninglessness of what he was doing. "The Old Capley grapevine is firing on all cylinders. The latest scuttlebutt is that Oliver Hawkhurst has been arrested."

"And charged?" Maltravers asked sharply.

"Don't know. He was seen being driven out of the park in a police car earlier this morning. However there's also a rumour that Luke Norman has vanished and the police are looking for him as well."

"Then you know just about everything that we do," said Maltravers. "Once they decide which one it is, it should be an open-and-shut case. We'll be back later."

As they walked down Bellringer Street to the Batsman, two police cars were still outside the Darbys' house and the street contained several groups of people taking carefully disguised interest. Opposite the cars a man on a stepladder was repairing a broken window.

"Heard about it then?" he asked as they reached him. "About Lord Dunford being murdered?" His day had clearly been considerably enlivened by the events and he was prepared to talk about it even to complete strangers.

"Yes, we've heard," Maltravers replied briefly.

"Bad business," the workman commented feelingly. "I liked Lord Dunford, he was a good boss."

"You work for the Estate then?"

"Yep. Lord and Lady P's very cut up about it and they've pulled in Mr Oliver for questioning. Never did like 'im." The man's tone indicated that this personal dislike of Hawkhurst had been instantly transmuted into a conviction of his guilt. Maltravers was disinclined to discuss the matter with a garrulous and morbidly fascinated workman standing opposite the house where it had occurred.

"What happened to the window?" he asked as they prepared to move on.

"Bloody drunks from the pub." The man gave the unlikely impression that hard drink was unknown to him. "It's always bleeding happening."

"The Estate owns this house then?"

"Yeah. Mr York and his wife live here. He sent me down to fix it."

Maltravers reflected that a broken window would have been a quite unnecessary added annoyance for Lord Pembury's secretary in the circumstances, but at least the Edenbridge workforce could be called on to replace it on a Sunday.

Run by a landlord with the attractive Pickwickian name of Juggins, the Batsman had survived more than two centuries of changing drinking habits without undue damage. The brewery chain that now owned it had renovated the premises without the tacky introduction of Space Invaders, jukebox, polystyrene mock beams, hideous plastic padding round the bar or half a ton

97

of brass wrought into imitation horse decorations and suspended against every upright surface. Polished wooden settles, honoured with time and fellowship, had been preserved, although they now stood on fitted carpet rather than congealed sawdust, and decrepit, pungent latrines had been replaced by modern plumbing. Maltravers' only complaint was his standard one, that he had to ask for his pint to be served in a traditional dimpled jug rather than the ubiquitous straight glass which he regarded, like electric organs, as part of the continuing curse of Cain upon mankind. He ordered their food, then carried his pint and Tess's whisky and water to where she was sitting by a striking stone fireplace, recently rescued from behind a Victorian plastering operation carried out for no apparent reason. The pub was full of talk and the talk was of nothing but murder.

Half-listening, Maltravers gathered that Hawkhurst's widely reported departure in a police car appeared to be regarded as much more significant than the parallel search for Luke Norman. Several slanderous remarks made by the customers in the lounge bar indicated that killing for financial gain was a very plausible motive, which cast a revealing light on the mores of Bellringer Street. Their food was brought to their table and they had just started eating when they were approached by a young man with the face of a starving ferret.

"Excuse me," he said. "I'm from the *Sun*."

"Welcome to our planet," Maltravers replied cordially. "Have a drink."

"Pardon?" The reporter seemed to be working out whether or not he had been insulted. Maltravers wondered how many more of his breed had been despatched at high speed to Old Capley for sensational, seamy and preferably sexy titbits that could be blown up out of all proportion. The excesses of parts of his previous profession had been something he had been very happy to leave behind.

"I don't think we can help you very much," he added. "We're strangers round here."

"Oh." Terrified that the opposition were even then working on an exclusive angle he had missed, the journalist feared another blind alley of inquiry. "You don't know about the murder then?"

"We know there's *been* a murder," Maltravers admitted. "And I heard somebody mention that the man who runs the local sex shop has been arrested."

Tess choked on a mouthful of Stilton as the reporter's face lit up like a man offered the Holy Grail of a Page One byline.

"What sex shop?" he demanded eagerly.

"I presume it must be the one in the square at the bottom of the hill," Maltravers replied. "Sells kinky underwear and that sort of thing."

"Who told you?" There was a hint of anxiety in the question.

"Someone at the bar mentioned it a few minutes ago." Maltravers was keeping his lying within the bounds of plausibility. "A chap from . . . which paper was it, darling? . . . the *Mirror*, I think, went off with him. I think they – " He stopped and grinned wickedly as the reporter fled with a frantic yelp of thanks.

"That was very unkind," Tess protested, still half laughing.

Maltravers distastefully watched the running outline of the journalist flash past the window of the pub and down the hill.

"On the day the *Belgrano* was sunk off the Falklands," he remarked, "the *Sun* gave a prize of a fiver and a tin of corned beef to a schoolboy who'd sent in a joke about Argentinians being killed. People who choose to work for papers like that deserve everything they get. He'll find out that it's a false lead soon enough."

He turned his attention back to his beer and Sunday ploughman's lunch. "However, I fear that Bellringer Street and its neighbourhood are going to become acutely aware of the disadvantages of a free Press over the next few days. Upper-class murder, middle-class respectability and – it's certain to come out – homosexuality. What more could any News Editor ask for in the silly season?"

Chapter Seven

It is a fact universally acknowledged among policemen that, having executed their crime, murderers do not then considerately take the trouble to search out a perfectly clean, smooth surface at the scene and carefully press all their fingers and thumbs on it to leave a convenient set of pristine prints; indeed, even single good impressions are not always found. However, fingermarks from various parts of the hand are usually revealed by a visitation of aluminium dust, and the room in which Dunford had been killed contained nineteen such different marks, offering confusion rather than possible leads. The sticky tape on the carpet had garnered a considerable collection of dust and other fragmentary bits and pieces, any one of which might prove invaluable, but only when the police had a definite, chargeable suspect.

On Sunday afternoon Detective Chief Superintendent Keith Miller surveyed the results of the forensic examination impassively, then turned to the medical report drawn up after the post-mortem. Stripped of its medical jargon, it said that Dunford had died after being hit a number of times – probably four – with a hard object on the left side of the head, damaging flesh and bone sufficiently to cause fatal damage to the brain; the pathologist noted that the skull had been markedly thinner than average. Detailed examination of the wound had revealed ridged patterns on the skin corresponding to the stitching round a cricket ball and the angle of blows suggested someone at least as tall as the deceased. The strength that would have been required indicated a man or an unusually powerful woman.

Miller leaned back in the chair that seemed too big for his bantamweight frame – he had only qualified for the police by a fraction of an inch in his height – and his narrow, inverted triangle face somehow managed to contract even further as he considered the situation, the pencil-thin moustache almost bridging the space between his cheeks. Three of the party guests had already indicated their intention of calling in their lawyers, and one had complained to the Chief Constable about the manner in which police inquiries at the house had been conducted. None of this concerned Miller; having served for a period on the Fraud Squad he was accustomed to outbursts of defensive outrage from allegedly respectable citizens when their affairs came under police scrutiny; the complaint he would just have to live with.

"So what have we got?" he said to David Parry. "Mr Hawkhurst is denying everything and his lawyer – Lord Pembury's family solicitor no less – is becoming increasingly tetchy. That gentleman must be handled carefully, incidentally. Meanwhile our Mr Norman has done a runner. What do you think?"

The fourth son of a Parks Attendant with Capley District Council, Parry had been born, bred and conditioned by life in the New Town and regarded Old Capley as an alien world populated by toffee-nosed, stinking-rich snobs. A constant lack of money in his childhood had made that commodity very important to him.

"It's got to be Hawkhurst," he said positively. "He had opportunity, motive and he ran."

"Not very far," Miller observed. "His story is that after the party he spent the rest of the night having it off in a house less than thirty yards away – we'll have to see what the lady concerned has to say about that – then he walked straight into us. As for opportunity, just about everybody in the house had that."

"Yes, but he's skint," Parry argued. "He's up to his ears in debt and now he stands to inherit a fortune."

"And it's all a bit obvious, isn't it?" objected Miller. "If he really wanted to kill Dunford – and I accept he's got reason to welcome his death – wouldn't he have planned it a bit better? He's not all that bright but is he such a complete wally? If I'd committed murder, I wouldn't jump into bed with some randy bit I'd only just met and hope she'd give me an alibi. I'll reserve judgment until we find out what Mrs Harriet Harper has to say, but I don't see Hawkhurst as our man at the moment. Someone's seeing her now, aren't they?"

"Sergeant Horne's round there," Parry confirmed. "But if it isn't Hawkhurst, it must be this poof Norman."

Miller sighed. "Sergeant, there are at least three senior officers in this county's force who are, to my knowledge, what you refer to as poofs and I've heard you speak very highly of two of them."

Parry looked resentful as his superior casually exposed another facet of his prejudices.

"However, Mr Norman does interest me," Miller continued. "This doesn't look like a murder that was planned in advance and a fit of passion after too much to drink looks very possible. And Mr Norman certainly appears to have done a runner."

As the two men spoke, reports had been received by Capley CID saying that Norman, whose MG had gone from Edenbridge House by the time the police arrived, was not at his flat above the Richmond antique shop and efforts to trace him were continuing.

"What do we do then?" Parry asked.

"Keep collecting evidence," Miller said simply. "We've not got enough to charge Hawkhurst – or anyone else for that matter – at the moment. We should have a statement from this Harper woman fairly soon and in the meantime we concentrate on finding those missing cricket balls. There's no sign of them in the house or the garden and we've started searching the churchyard, right? Keep me informed."

Parry left the room unsatisfied. His basic hostility towards the rich and privileged had been amplified by Hawkhurst's imperious behaviour – the smooth London lawyer had thrown in some belittling remarks about provincial police forces as well – hardening it into a desire that he should be guilty. He was privately inclined to coax a confession out of him by methods generally frowned upon by the defenders of civil liberties. He returned to the incident room to read another report that continuing inquiries among Luke Norman's family and known friends had still not traced him.

"This is intolerable!"

Sunday-school teacher, parish councillor and primary-school governor Harriet Harper glared at Sergeant Kate Horne with inflamed fury.

"Sergeant, I must warn you that if the police repeat such an offensive suggestion, then I shall seek legal advice and take the most serious action. I do *not* casually go to bed with men I happen to meet at parties!"

She sat in the high-backed wicker chair, arms folded defensively in front of her as Kate Horne looked back impassively.

"I'm sure you appreciate that we must investigate what Mr Hawkhurst has told us, Mrs Harper," she said. "He is being questioned in connection with a murder and claims he was with you in this house at the time. If that is true, it could eliminate him from our inquiries. Are you saying that he never came to this house last night?"

Harriet Harper turned away evasively, biting her lip in fury. Hawkhurst had been a gauche and incompetent bed partner; now he was using the incident to provide himself with an alibi. After a moment's hesitation, she looked at the sergeant again defiantly.

"He did not!"

"I see. Thank you." Kate Horne pulled a notebook out of the

pocket of her suit. "And are you prepared to make an official statement to that effect, Mrs Harper?"

"If it's absolutely necessary, yes," she snapped.

"Very well." The sergeant paused as she took out her pen and unscrewed the top. "Of course you realise that if Mr Hawkhurst continues to claim he was here, the police may have to send forensic experts to examine your bedroom? Just to settle the matter beyond argument."

Harriet Harper stared at her. "Are you saying the police will not accept my word?"

"In the circumstances, I'm afraid not. If Mr Hawkhurst persists with his story, his lawyer will certainly insist we investigate in any event."

The woman looked at her apprehensively. "Surely I could object?"

"Yes, but we would secure a warrant if necessary. I'm sorry, Mrs Harper, but the police would have no choice in the matter."

"And what would you expect to find?"

Kate Horne shrugged. "A number of things. Hair on the pillow, fingerprints perhaps, traces of sweat . . ." She smiled innocently. "And other secretions. We would of course notice if all the bed linen had been changed."

For several seconds the two women stared at each other, then Harriet Harper lowered her eyes in defeat.

"Mr Hawkhurst came to my house after the party. Is that enough for you?"

"Thank you, Mrs Harper, we don't need all the details. Your private life is not the concern of the police." Kate Horne held her pen against a page of the notebook. "Can you tell me what time he arrived?"

"One-fifteen."

The sergeant looked up sharply. "Are you quite certain of that, Mrs Harper?"

Harriet Harper gestured towards a mahogany grandmother clock in the corner of the front room where they were sitting.

"It had just chimed the quarter hour when he came in," she said.

"And how long before that did you leave the party?"

"I'm not certain. About twenty minutes, perhaps half an hour."

"And Mr Hawkhurst was still in the house when you left?"

"Yes."

Kate Horne reported back to the inspector in charge of the incident room an hour later.

"She admitted it finally," she said. "But didn't we get the first call about the murder at one-eighteen? I thought so. Then according to Harper's statement, Hawkhurst could have been in that house up to only a few minutes earlier. It doesn't look much of an alibi to me."

Early on Sunday evening, the police released a photograph of Luke Norman, which they had found in his flat, to the media. Despite a carefully-worded statement that they only wanted to question him in order to eliminate him from their inquiries – the customary oblique phrase they would use if they wanted to talk to Hitler about World War II – the press devoured it hungrily. One of London's most famous homosexuals made a good deal of money tipping off several reporters about Dunford's hitherto unsuspected private life and, unfettered by someone being inconveniently charged (which would have severely restricted their behaviour), the tabloids deliriously plunged into a sea of scandal. "Queer peer's boyfriend in murder hunt" was one of the more restrained headlines.

Alister York was not mad, but he had been hideously damaged by a father who recognised no other way to bring up his children than by brutality. Childish tears of disappointment, poor marks at school, the playful waywardness of a small boy, had all brought the same vicious physical reprisals. The buckle end of a belt, a stinging cane across the knuckles, deliberate slaps across the head, had hammered York into a distorted shape. He did not hate his father; the pain and terror had been warped into an unquestioning acceptance and respect. He was contemptuous of those who paraded similar terrors from their childhood and wanted sympathy; they had been broken and had not deserved the advantages of a strong parent. Where others had hatred and bitterness, he had a perverse admiration and could now joke with the retired senior Civil Servant in Hastings about moments of rage and assault that had become the twisted remembered joys of infancy. Father and son now shared the same attitudes; simple bullies who could see only virtue in their savagery. York's mother's suicide they could only comprehend as the ultimate weakness of a woman who could not cope with reality. As secretary to Lord Pembury, York was conscientious, honest and diligent; to those who worked under him he was demanding but efficient; to his friends he was cordial but cold; to his wife he was an iron tyrant.

On Sunday evening, Joanna York became aware that her husband was staring at her as she embroidered tiny, meticulous stitches into a pattern of leaves on a linen tablecloth. Feeling the weight of his eyes across the room, she looked up inquiringly.

"What is it?" she asked, and when the stony expression on his face did not change, she felt apprehensive. Somehow she had displeased him and her best defence would be not to argue, which would only inflame his displeasure into terrifying, crushing temper. She could not imagine what she might have inadvertently done.

"I was just thinking how well you're controlling your feelings," he said.

"My feelings?" she said cautiously, looking down as she started to weave her needle in and out of the cloth again. "What about?" Her mind was racing, trying to work out what he meant.

"About the death of your lover, the handsome Lord Dunford."

The needle twitched and a spot of blood dropped on to the emerald stitching. It was a reaction of shock and amazement, but York regarded it as proof; it took him less than an hour to break her.

A few doors away in Bellringer Street, Maltravers and Tess felt that they were stepping with extreme care around a great hole as Peter and Susan gingerly probed the gaping wound that had appeared in their marriage. The difficulties caused by almost every casual remark carrying suspected overtones had been curiously relieved by Dunford's murder; gently telling Timmy and Emma that Uncle Simon was dead was actually preferable to trying to behave normally before the children went to bed. Maltravers turned on the television and the four of them saw Luke Norman's face staring from the screen as the voice-over said that police were still looking for him.

"Have they released Oliver then?" Peter wondered.

"Well they certainly haven't charged him," said Maltravers, "or they wouldn't be looking so hard for Luke. It looks like they have two high-level suspects and spot the red herring. Even if they have released cousin Oliver they can always pull him in again. It will all depend on what Luke has to say when he turns up."

"Which one do you think it was?" Susan asked.

Maltravers shrugged. "My first instincts were that it was Luke because of what we knew, and his disappearance tends to convince me I'm right. But I'm not about to produce brilliant Marpellian theories about stolen ties and missing cricket balls which will neatly explain everything."

"You must have thought about them though," said Tess. "It's like some obscure crossword clue that would appeal to you."

Maltravers produced one of the rare smiles seen in the house that evening. "All right, I've tried. I have the feeling that if those odd matters could be explained a lot more would become clear. But I'm sure the police will sort it out with mundane questioning and procedures. Eccentric speculation will play no part in it. I know truth can be stranger than fiction, but most of the time it's much less interesting."

Drained by her own denials, Joanna York sat numbed and defeated, driven almost to believe the lies that had warped her innocence into guilt. She sat like a rabbit in the shadow of a great dog as York loomed over her.

"That's better," he said quietly. "I knew you'd confess it in the end."

Her head shook feebly; she had confessed nothing because there had been nothing to confess. In her weary submission, she felt a final flicker of defiance as her sense of shame became intolerable. She summoned up some last reserve of anger.

"No!" she cried bitterly. "No, no, no! It wasn't like that! He only . . . Oh God, I hate you!"

Alister York hit her. Not in rage but with the casual indifference a man would use to swat a fly. As the shocking sting of the blow crashed through her head, the last glimmer of Joanna's resistance died.

"You're lying," he said dismissively. "Aren't you? Admit it."

As her spirit crumbled, Joanna York actually began to believe that she might have been lying. The warm memory of Dunford paying her attention and being kind before that meaningless kiss under the Christmas mistletoe at Edenbridge House had become twisted into something shameful and dirty.

"I'm sorry," she whimpered. "I didn't mean . . ." The remnants of her voice faded. It will stop now, she thought, now I've admitted it. Don't let him hit me again.

"Very well," said York. "It's time we went up to bed."

It had not stopped, it had only just begun.

It was half past three in the morning when Maltravers gave a series of Cro-Magnon grunts as Tess urgently shook him awake.

"Gus!" she insisted. "Wake up!"

Maltravers' consciousness began to emerge hazily through a further collection of inarticulate sounds.

"What is it?" he demanded tetchily.

"The baby. It's on the way. Get up. I'm going back to help."

Satisfied she had roused him beyond retreat back into sleep, Tess left the room and Maltravers blinked owlishly at the ceiling for a few moments before rolling out of bed and pulling on his dressing gown. He had grasped the situation and did not like it. He paused on the landing where the sound of anxious voices and mysterious activity from Peter and Susan's room convinced him that his presence there would be both useless and inconvenient. Downstairs in the kitchen he filled the electric kettle, turned it on and was listening to its rising murmur with growing misgivings as Tess reappeared.

"What on earth are you doing?"

"Boiling water of course," he said. "I've never known what it's for, but I understand it's required in large quantities at such times."

"Well, if you want to scald the poor thing to death it might be useful," said Tess. "Don't you know *anything* about babies?"

"Enough to recognise one at fifty paces which had always seemed a safe distance," he replied, then waved uncertainly at the kettle. "Anyway, don't things have to be sterilised or something?"

"It's too late for that," Tess told him. "Junior's arrived."

"Arrived?" Maltravers looked round in alarm, as though expecting the diminutive Penrose to appear through the kitchen door at any moment with demands of post-natal attention. "Where's the ambulance? Why hasn't she been taken to hospital?"

"It's a bit late for that. He's here and he's fine." Tess kissed him on the cheek. "Anyway, you can make us all a cup of tea. I do love you when you're being helpless."

Peter and Susan's third child had arrived with what

Maltravers later held to be indecent haste. When Susan had punched her husband awake about half an hour earlier to say the baby was coming, he had automatically got up and started dressing to take her to Capley General Hospital. He had just pulled on his underpants when Susan had sharply added that she had meant exactly what she had said – the baby was not only coming, he had virtually arrived. Having witnessed the births of both his other children and with an ability in practical matters which Maltravers did not share, Peter had grabbed towels from the airing cupboard and set to work. Woken by the disturbance, Tess had joined in with encouraging noises and her hand had been squeezed very tightly as the population of Old Capley increased by a male child, weighing, as it later transpired, a healthy seven and a half pounds.

Maltravers entered the bedroom carrying a tray with some trepidation, anxious lest he should tread in something unidentifiable and probably slippery. Back in bed from her delivery on the floor, Susan was clutching the baby protectively in a blanket with Tess sitting beside her. Peter had gone downstairs to telephone the doctor.

"Come and see him, Gus. He's beautiful," Susan said.

Maltravers cautiously crossed the room and looked down at a tiny head which appeared to have been carved from a beetroot by a reasonably accomplished child and wondered if so much hair was usual.

"Beautiful," he repeated obediently.

Susan was making no effort to hold back her tears and there was relief and joy in her voice as she looked at her second son.

"He's Peter's," she said. "It looks just like him. You can see that, can't you Gus?"

Maltravers recalled that when Lewis Carroll was asked for an opinion by doting parents of the very young, he would peer intently into the bassinet then announce, "Ah, now that *is* a baby", an anodyne formula that appeared to satisfy everyone.

Normally he would personally venture no further, but when Susan looked at him he knew what he had to say.

"Yes, it looks like Peter. Does he have a name?"

"I don't know," said Susan. "I haven't thought about that, just about . . ." She broke off and gulped emotionally. "Perhaps we'll call him Augustus. After all, you were here when he was born."

"Hardly," Maltravers contradicted. "I was taking evasive action. Think about it later."

Susan's eyes flashed past him to the door as Peter returned.

"Doctor's on the way," he announced. "He's arranging an ambulance to take you both to hospital but I've told him everything's fine. How is he?"

He crossed to the bed and Susan held the baby towards him and he took the bundle of warm, fluffy towel from her.

"Daddy didn't make a bad job of helping you arrive, did he?" he said.

It was, Maltravers felt, a singularly happy place to be as Peter cuddled his son and tears of anything but unhappiness ran down his wife's face. Their marriage was on the mend and there was no more sleep for any of them that night.

Joanna York did not sleep either, but for very different reasons.

Chapter Eight

On Monday morning, his inappropriately smiling photograph staring from the front pages of some fifteen million copies of national newspapers, Luke Norman's face was temporarily among the best known in Britain. Awareness of him was constantly multiplied by regional evening papers and inescapable, repeated flashes on television screens. Unbelievably, more than twenty people failed to recognise him as he left a flat in Chiswick and walked the hundred yards to his car. The flat belonged to one of his former lovers who was on holiday and to whom Norman had omitted to return the key when their affair had ended; it had been a secure, brief sanctuary while he tried to sort out the turmoil in his mind.

The previous evening he had sat and watched the television with a sense of numbed disbelief as he looked at his own face and half heard the news reporter describing his appearance and his car. The bare essentials of the police wanting to question him about Simon's murder were all that remained in his memory; the shots of the closed antique shop and the carefully phrased comments on his life and sexual tendencies he had forgotten as unimportant. Now he wanted nothing more than to go somewhere where he could be alone with his torment. The police would certainly be tracing his known associates, so the flat would have to be abandoned. As he drove round the M25 circling London towards the M4 and the West Country, the dead man he had loved was a spectral presence in the passenger seat; in the car's glove compartment was a programme for *La Cage aux Folles*, a heart-twisting reminder of a night out together.

The motorway unwound before him, a tedious strip of streaming road as successive southern counties approached and retreated. He stopped for petrol and to buy some sandwiches at Leigh Delamere service station – another group of people who looked at him with indifference if at all – then he drove on through Somerset and Devon and into Cornwall as if only the final end of land would make him stop and face the nightmare of it all. The simple act of driving was an escape into another escape until there would be no more escape left.

The motorway ended and he went on westwards, through market towns and villages, brushing past holiday resorts, across moors and between low, swelling hills. The road took him into Penzance with St Michael's Mount glowing like terracotta in the early evening sunshine, then he followed the narrowing way along the final ragged edges of the peninsula, through Newlyn and Mousehole, now taking every dwindling turn that offered him the promise of further road. He dropped down the steep approach to Lamorna Cove and finally stopped in the little car park overlooking the sea. He had been driving mindlessly for so long that the enforced cessation of movement momentarily confused him and he sat with the engine still running, staring blindly at the shallow waves of the Atlantic lapping softly over the stones on the beach. He was four hundred miles from Bellringer Street but there was no deliverance. As a hawking seagull landed on the wall in front of him and turned its cruelly-beaked face towards the car, Luke Norman leaned against the steering wheel and wept.

Despite their apparent health, Susan and the baby had been taken into hospital for checks and Tess had volunteered to take on the household while she was away. As Maltravers walked with her down Bellringer Street to the butcher's shop in the square, complete strangers, somehow already aware of the news, stopped them with constant questions. The innocence of a new baby was balm to the wounds of shock, distaste and discomfort Old Capley was feeling in the light of that morning's papers. Trying to remember a whole series of names of people sending congratulations, they joined the queue in the shop. Maltravers smiled and said good morning to Joanna York who was a couple of places in front of him, but she ignored him.

In an age of anonymous meat sealed in shining plastic wrappings, the Old Capley butcher still displayed his red and cream joints and carcasses on cold marble or hung from steel hooks. Such offerings remained a matter for discussion and critical appraisal and the woman at the front of the queue was examining a piece of silverside like a judge at Cruft's assessing a potential best in breed. Tess found it restful and rather quaint; Maltravers was mentally recording the conversation as the sort of dialogue that he rarely heard.

As the butcher waited, patient and attentive, the piece of meat was weighed in the hand, its fat content criticised, its capacity to serve six people questioned, its pedigree as first-class beef put under suspicion. Perhaps there was something else? A hand of pork? Possibly a crown roast? The butcher smiled and produced further offerings; it was not a shop for people in a hurry. Tess picked up a leaflet from a display stand and was asking Maltravers if he could think up an ingenious slogan – in not more than ten words – about the joys of eating sausages so that they could win a holiday in Florida, when Joanna York cracked. Everybody in the shop looked surprised as the girl whirled out of her place in the queue and almost ran out of the door, stifling a cry. Other customers seemed startled, even offended at such excessive public behaviour, but Maltravers and Tess glanced at each other in alarm then went after her as she hurried across the square back towards Bellringer Street. Maltravers caught her up within half a dozen paces and touched her shoulder.

"Are you all right?" he asked.

Tess reached them both as Joanna York turned to face him, tears pouring from eyes haunted not by grief or shock but what looked like stark terror. In an ordinary young woman outside a parade of shops on a summer's morning, it was like seeing death in a child's nursery.

"Go away! Please!" Joanna York choked out the words as she shook Maltravers' hand off her shoulder and turned away, now running as fast as she could up Bellringer Street. They stood and watched her as she reached her house and fumbled with the key, then the sound of the slamming door came down the empty street to them.

"What the hell's the matter with her?" said Maltravers. "She looks as though she's going mad."

"I'm going after her," said Tess.

"No." Maltravers took hold of Tess's arm to prevent her. "We hardly know the woman and if she's that upset, she's not going to welcome strangers turning up on her doostep."

"But we can't just leave her like that," Tess protested. "We're not strangers. You told me you talked to her at the party. For God's sake, Gus, she looks ready to kill herself! We've got to – "

"Just take your angel-of-mercy hat off for a moment and we'll compromise," Maltravers interrupted. "Go and see her later on. She's too upset at the moment, but she may have calmed down in a while."

Tess looked back up the hill, fighting her instincts.

"All right," she said finally. "But we don't leave it too long."

"No, we don't," Maltravers agreed. "There's something very wrong there and I'd like to know what it is."

Anticipating various combinations of death, there were several defined lines of inheritance for the Pembury estate. Both of Lord Pembury's brothers were dead and his sister was unmarried and past child-bearing, leaving his nephew the only direct descendant after his son on his side of the family. Thereafter various members of Lady Pembury's family could inherit, but a direct male line stretching back to the return of the Stuarts was not to be broken unless absolutely unavoidable. In the circumstances, Sir Gerald Piers-Freeman found it most unsatisfactory that Oliver Hawkhurst should remain under police suspicion.

"Obviously your nephew could not inherit should he be found to be in any way implicated in Lord Dunford's death," he told Lord Pembury. "While clearly his innocence is presumed at this stage, it makes the position somewhat . . . delicate."

"What would you advise?" asked Pembury.

"As there appears to be . . ." Sir Gerald's smile was like a razor cut across paper, " . . . forgive me, no question of your own death being in any way imminent, Lord Pembury, I would suggest that we wait. Hopefully Mr Hawkhurst will be exonerated – or found guilty, we must accept that I'm afraid – which will clarify the situation. If that happens fairly speedily, matters should resolve themselves without any undue complications."

Pembury swivelled round in his study chair and looked out of the window at part of the formal gardens of Edenbridge House. His grief rigidly controlled, he was accepting his responsibilities of securing the future. He had been brought up from childhood with the insistence that the great house and all that it represented were his only in trust; the family was greater than any individual member of it. While he had never particularly liked his nephew – and now was reluctantly forced to consider the possibility that he might conceivably have murdered his son – he recognised the need to make certain arrangements as inescapable.

"Very well," he agreed at last. "And what is the precise position at present with regard to the police and my nephew? When will he be released?"

"Ah . . ." Sir Gerald's smooth, correct and professional manner was momentarily ruffled. "There appears to be a difficulty, temporary I am sure. Mr Hawkhurst told the police in my presence that he went to . . . visit another person in a house nearby after the party. Unfortunately, it transpires that the person concerned is adamant that he arrived at a time which would not have made it totally impossible for him to have committed the crime. It's most unfortunate, but I'm sure matters will soon be clarified. I have, of course, made it quite clear that unless the police prefer charges and bring Mr Hawkhurst before a magistrate by the appropriate time, I shall insist on his release."

Alister York, who was sitting on the other side of the desk, noticed that Lord Pembury's eyes were hooded beneath the lids, a well-known indication that he was growing angry.

"I see," he said after a long pause. "Thank you for your advice, Sir Gerald, and for your representation of my nephew."

The solicitor recognised the note of conclusion and tapped a sheaf of papers together on the desk top before replacing them in his briefcase. "My impression is that the police have nothing substantive in the way of evidence," he added. "There is nothing more than a supposed and quite outrageous motive. However . . ." he snapped the briefcase closed and looked at Lord Pembury blandly, " . . . it has occurred to me that the police do not appear to have had to make extensive inquiries to discover the extent of the financial difficulties with which Mr Hawkhurst is faced. In fact, they appear to have known about them almost from the beginning of their investigation, which . . . leads one to consider who might have informed them so quickly, don't you think?"

Sir Gerald removed his half-moon glasses and slipped them into a soft leather case as he looked interrogatively at Lord Pembury – then turned his bland gaze on York who stared at him for a moment before looking back cautiously at his employer.

"What are you suggesting, Sir Gerald?" Pembury asked.

"Merely that, if that is the case, it is something to which I might feel it necessary to draw the attention of the police once Mr Hawkhurst has been cleared of any involvement. It would be . . . interesting to know the motives of whoever afforded them the information."

York detested the man with his hyper-polished manner, probing suggestions and oh-so-smooth delivery; he lacked the courage to deliver his implications directly but was using York's presence in the room to wheedle something out like a rat worrying at a can on a trash heap. His insinuations made York decide to bring it into the open.

"Lord Pembury, I told the police about Mr Hawkhurst."

Sir Gerald's smile became that of an Inquisition priest hearing the dragged-out confession of a heretic.

"You told the police what about Mr Hawkhurst?" Pembury's hooded eyes were now almost closed.

"About his financial problems, that he had been refused further help from yourself and that on Lord Dunford's death he became your heir." York had no intention of giving Sir Gerald any further satisfaction by saying anything that could be construed as an apology for what he had done.

"And why did you think that was necessary?"

York could almost feel Sir Gerald squirming with pleasure as Pembury put the next question. He turned and looked defiantly at the solicitor before replying.

"Because they would eventually have found it out – and because it was clearly possible that Mr Hawkhurst could have committed the crime. He had every reason to – that very evening he had approached me about what help the Estate might still give him – and every opportunity. If I had not spoken, I could later have been accused of withholding relevant information. I'm sure Sir Gerald can appreciate the legal position that could have left me in."

The lawyer turned his face away with the dismissive expression of a politician who does not choose to acknowledge a valid point made by the other side.

"Why have you not told me this before?" Pembury asked quietly.

"I've not had the opportunity. I'm sorry, but . . ." York cursed himself for using the word, but it was too late, " . . . I was in a position in which I had no alternative. Naturally I trust that Mr Hawkhurst is innocent."

"Oh, naturally." Sir Gerald's whisper was so soft it was difficult to be sure that he had spoken.

"Please be so good as to inform me in future of any further action you may feel . . . obliged to take in this matter. Thank you, Alister, that will be all for the moment."

The study clock ticked ten times in the silence before York stood up and left the room. Back in his office he slammed the file he was carrying on to his desk and stood by the window, angry, heaving breath clouding the glass. He had been so certain that suspicion would fall on Hawkhurst, so convinced that what he had told the police would result in a murder charge. And it was still possible. From what the lawyer had said, Hawkhurst's alibi had been found wanting and he was not yet in the clear. York's mind wrestled with the problem of what further evidence he might be able to produce that would damn him – and wipe the sneering smile off Sir Gerald's haughty face.

Maltravers and Tess went to the Batsman again for lunch, where the previously unknown relationship between Dunford and Luke Norman had given the bar-room regulars considerable material for discussion, revealing an interesting mixed reaction towards such behaviour. The prevailing view appeared to be that anyone who played a decent game of cricket could be forgiven certain private habits, although you should keep an eye on them in the shower room after the match. Luke Norman, on the other hand, was too damned pretty for a man, was not known to be a cricketer and had more or less admitted everything by going into hiding. Waiting to be served, Maltravers listened, half-amused, half-appalled.

"The clever money seems to be on Luke now," he remarked as he rejoined Tess. "Although prejudice is running riot all over the place."

"I'm not too concerned about that at the moment," Tess replied. "I'm more worried about what's the matter with Joanna York."

"It could, of course, be just that she's upset at Simon's murder, but . . ." Maltravers thought back and shook his head in rejection. "No, it was more than that. Even if there had been something between them – which is quite possible from everything we now know about Simon – why should she look so terrified? Unless, of course . . . Alister York?" Tess nodded as he looked across the table at her inquiringly.

"Oh, yes," she said. "I'm ahead of you. He's highly over-possessive and certainly the jealous type. It wouldn't have taken much of a flirtation by Simon to make him angry – and I think he could be very angry indeed. Which means that he could have done it and now she's terrified because he's told her and she's too scared to go to the police. Christ, it's plausible Gus."

"Horribly plausible," agreed Maltravers. "You're not ahead of me, you've just said what I've been thinking. But what the hell can we do?"

"Go to the police."

"But the trouble is we don't *know* anything," Maltravers objected. "We've come up with a theory after seeing Joanna York suffering from some sort of terminal panic, but that doesn't mean we can start accusing her husband of murder. We've already pointed the police in Luke Norman's direction. They're going to start getting ideas about us if we come up with somebody else as well without some hard evidence."

But Maltravers knew the theory was disturbingly persuasive. York had found Dunford's body – or at least had said he had, which was a well-known smokescreen – and it was irresistibly possible that he could have killed him. Maltravers recalled that York had said he was looking for Dunford to say goodnight when he found him dead; the story suddenly sounded very thin. He took a pensive mouthful of bitter.

"How can we find out anything more?" he wondered.

"I'll go and see her and try and get her to talk," said Tess.

"It's worth a try. Do you want me to come too?"

"No. I don't think she's very comfortable with men. No woman with a husband like that would be. And two of us would probably frighten her as well. It'll be best if I go on my own."

They finished their lunch hastily and walked back up Bellringer Street, where Tess stopped for a moment outside the York's house until Maltravers had disappeared round the corner at the top of the hill before she rang the bell. There was no reply at first, but she was convinced Joanna York was still in the house and kept ringing until the curtains at the front window moved slightly, then the door was opened a couple of inches.

"Yes? What is it?"

Only part of the girl's face was visible, apprehensive and enquiring. Tess said nothing; had she asked to go in, she was sure of instant refusal and the slender opening she was being offered would close. She summoned up every feeling of sympathy she could find and put it across in her silent face; for several seconds the two women looked at each other, then the door opened just a fraction more.

"I'm all right," Joanna said, but there was no conviction in her voice. "I wasn't well this morning. I'm sorry if I . . ."

Softly, softly, thought Tess. "Don't apologise. You're looking much better now. We were just a bit concerned, that's all."

Joanna York was not looking better. Her make-up was fresh and her hair was combed – but what Tess and Maltravers had seen earlier remained in the eyes.

"If you're not feeling well, I'll be happy to get your shopping for you," she added. "You obviously wanted something from the butcher."

"No, it's all right . . . I'll do it later." She was rapidly backing off.

"Well, if you're sure. It's really no trouble." Tess tried the only opening she could think of. "Actually I'm getting to know your local shops. You've heard about Susan's baby I suppose?"

Now she was just someone calling with a piece of village news, not an intruder. But the door did not open any further.

"No. What's happened?"

"He arrived in the middle of the night. Great dramas."

"Oh. How nice. Give them my love. Thank you for telling me. Would you excuse me? I've got something on the stove."

Wrong, lady, all bloody wrong, thought Tess as the words rattled meaninglessly out, the smile flashed automatically and the door swiftly shut. No woman – and not many men – would dismiss such an announcement so hastily. No questions, no interest, no surprise, just a big, fat nothing. Don't try and tell me you're all right. For a few moments she stared at the door in frustration then hurried back to the Penroses.

"Well?" Maltravers asked urgently as she walked into the kitchen. "Did you find out anything?"

"Nothing and everything," she replied. "You can't get through to her. I told her about Susan's baby and it was as if I'd said there was something good on television tonight. We *are* on to something, darling."

"Yes, but what? It could be that . . . I don't know . . . that she's been told she's got cancer or something. We've got to accept that there are other possibilities – perhaps more likely ones – than that her husband is a murderer." Maltravers sighed. "But it's still possible . . . Perhaps we could talk to a friend of hers?"

"From what Susan told us, she doesn't appear to have all that many," said Tess. "Susan might know but . . . look, Simon was murdered when? The early hours of Sunday morning. Today we see Joanna York looking like a madwoman. All right, the two things may not be connected, but it's one hell of a coincidence. Susan's in hospital and we don't know anyone else in Old Capley to talk to about Joanna York. We have a perfectly realistic theory that says her husband could have killed Simon. What do we *do*?"

Maltravers made a sound of frustration. "The best thing I can suggest is that you try again later, but . . . let me think a minute . . . you can't just go back with the obvious intention of wanting to make her talk, we need some excuse for you to get into the house. Any ideas?"

"I'll find something," Tess promised him. "Believe me. Because the more I think about it, the more certain I am that we really have come up with someone else with a motive to kill Simon."

"I know we have," said Maltravers. "And I wish I could find some reason to stop thinking that we're right. Because if we are, it also means that Joanna York is in danger."

Chapter Nine

Dunford was dead and Alister York knew his career at Edenbridge House had finished, but he would conscientiously continue to carry out his duties until the end of his final day there. Having placed the death notice in *The Times* and discussed the funeral arrangements with the vicar of St Barbara's and the local undertaker, he drafted out the wording of an invitation. While it was certain that the church would be packed for the burial of Lord Dunford, only certain selected people would be invited back to the house; the strictest conventions of etiquette walked with the Pemburys to the grave. He wrote the draft swiftly, his fountain pen – he abhorred ballpoint pens – sweeping in a strong, italic script over the paper; thirty years earlier his father had forged those classic pothooks by standing behind him, chillingly tapping a steel ruler against his hand as his son agonisingly practised and perfected them.

Lord Pembury looked up coldly as York knocked softly on the study door and walked in with the draft in his hand. He took it without a word, read it through in silence then handed it back.

"Arrange for one hundred to be printed once the date has been confirmed," he said. "I shall let you have a list of those to whom they are to be sent."

"Yes, Lord Pembury." York opened a desk diary he had brought with him. "I was unable to discuss this while Sir Gerald was here. You have appointments on Wednesday and Thursday, one at Edenbridge, the other with the Liberal

124

leader at the House of Lords. Do you wish me to cancel them?"

"No. However, Lady Pembury will not be meeting engagements for the time being. The household staff are to wear mourning until after the funeral, but that does not apply to the tourists' guides. If they wish to wear black ties or something similar, that is a matter for them. The flag will be flown at half-mast until Lord Dunford has been buried. His body will remain in the chapel of the house after its release by the coroner until it is taken to the church. Only family flowers will be accepted at the house, all others must be sent to the undertakers.

"Once the date of the funeral has been settled, advertise that Edenbridge House and Park will be closed for the day. The police must also be advised of those attending for whom security precautions will be necessary. The family and principal mourners will walk to the church."

York made rapid and neat notes as Lord Pembury dispassionately gave instructions regarding the burial of his son; personal tragedy dealt with by duty and tradition. Edenbridge House had seen many deaths and the machinery for dealing with them was unalterable.

"These letters have arrived which require your attention." York passed across a leather folder as Pembury finished speaking. "I assumed you would wish to deal with them. I will of course handle all household matters unless something urgent arises."

Pembury placed the folder on his desk. "I'll read them later and draft replies. Is there anything further?"

"No, Lord Pembury."

"Thank you."

Pembury returned his attention to a biography of Joseph Kennedy, another man who had buried sons. York hesitated as if to say something else, then turned and walked towards the door.

"There was an advertisement in *Horse and Hound* last week for a personal secretary to the Duke of Bray," Pembury said without looking up. "I don't know if you noticed it."

York paused for half a step then walked on without responding. It was a very gentlemanly way of being fired.

Coincidentally, at around the same time, Miller and his murder team were bouncing ideas round in their incident room as statements from everybody at the party – confused, half-remembered and generally useless – were collated and fed into a computer.

"Lateral thinking time," said Miller. "Chummy's alibi from the lady doesn't stand up but we've got nothing strong enough to hold him on and he's being released with his lawyer's assurance that he will be available if we want to talk to him again. There's still no sign of the elusive Mr Norman. Question: could it have been somebody else? There were twenty-seven people in that house when we arrived, remember."

"What about this chap . . . what's his name? . . . York?" said one detective. "He couldn't wait to point the finger at Hawkhurst, could he? Not the sort of thing you'd expect from a faithful private secretary. And he's the one who found the body."

Miller frowned all over his face. "Definite possibility. Frankly, my money's still on Norman, but until we find him and see what he has to say for himself it's a good point . . . just keep an eye on Mr York."

Maltravers and Tess looked through the immense wrought-iron gates of St Barbara's as they left the Penroses for a walk in the park. The gates were guarded by a uniformed policeman and inside they could see more men, several with dogs, probing between the gravestones and in the bushes.

"Hunt the cricket ball, I presume," said Maltravers. "If one of those turns up complete with tell-tale fingerprints all our questions may be answered. One assumes it must have been the weapon. But who wielded it?"

"I'd like to go in the church again," said Tess. "Where Simon took me. I suppose we can't at the moment."

"I don't think they'll take kindly to tourists just now. But it shouldn't take them long to finish in there – it's not all that big." Maltravers started walking towards the Bellringer Street gate into the Park. "Tell me about that visit again."

Tess found the memory painful. Only hours before he had died, Simon had been amused and amusing and had revealed to her something of his secret self; when she was able to go back into the church it might be a catharsis.

"I told you most of it," she said. "Oh, except for one silly story."

Maltravers listened in amusement to the strange tale of the dead butler killed by a free-falling Earl of Pembury.

"What a very odd skeleton in the cupboard," he remarked. "Which reminds me, I wonder if there's any news about the lost remains of Tom Bostock? Probably not, there are much more serious matters now. What about that other grave that Simon showed you? Susannah or somebody? Where's that?"

"Just near the door to the Darbys' garden. That was just horrible."

"She was a very unfortunate girl," he agreed. "And now we know exactly why Simon identified with her."

"But for God's sake, it was different for him," objected Tess. Maltravers shook his head.

"Not really. Simon suffered the dreadful burden of primogeniture. Everything – the title, the wealth and the privileges – must go to the eldest son and in his case he was the only son. And he would have had to marry and produce an heir to follow him."

"Tell me, what date do they have on the damned calendars at Edenbridge House?" Tess demanded angrily. "Do they know it's the twentieth century? You're describing a bloody feudal system."

"Perhaps, but it works. Without it, the great estates and houses of England would have been splintered within a few generations. There'd be nowhere like this," Maltravers gestured all around as they entered the lodge gates to the park, with the house visible through the trees. "No Longleat or Beaulieu or any of them. The monarchy works on the same principle. We'd have a king for every county if everything had to be divided up fairly between the children all the time. It's nothing to do with fairness, it's a matter of preservation. Simon recognised it and was trapped by it."

"But now some other member of the family – possibly Oliver – will inherit and the result's the same," said Tess. "Simon said he couldn't refuse the title but he could have done if he'd really wanted to. Edward VIII gave up the throne – and he did it for love, remember."

"And look what happened," said Maltravers. "He alienated his family, nearly wrecked the system and forced his brother to take on the burden for him: a burden that eventually killed him. Very romantic, but very wrong according to the rules. Simon was a stronger man than that. It hurt him, just like it hurt Susannah all those years ago, but he would not let the family down. You may think it's stupid – a lot of people would – but it's an honourable stupidity."

"Susannah Hawkhurst killed herself because of that honourable stupidity," Tess said bitterly.

"As I said before: ancient aristocracy, different rules." Maltravers took Tess's hand sympathetically. "How very strange it all is. Right, which way shall we go?"

"Not too far. I want to get back to try and see Joanna York again. I've got an excuse which I think will work."

"Let's just stroll up and look at the house again then. That won't take long."

Edenbridge Park was crowded again, although there were fewer people about than when they had been there the previous Friday or during the cricket match. Maltravers was taking some photographs of Tess with Edenbridge House in the background when he suddenly lowered the camera and looked beyond her.

"Hello," he said. "It's the 'orrible Oliver."

Tess turned and saw Hawkhurst getting out of a taxi in front of the house.

"So the police must have released him," she said. "Does that mean he's in the clear?"

"Maybe. Or it could just mean they haven't charged him and can't hold him any longer or . . . I wonder? Have they found Luke Norman? Come on, let's get back and see if there's anything on the radio about it."

They were just about to go back into the Penroses' house when Maltravers stopped and looked across at the church again.

"What was that story Simon told you about the butler?" he asked.

"Butler?" said Tess. "You remember, he was killed when Lord Pembury fell on him. Why?"

"There was something . . ." Maltravers' eyes narrowed as if he was trying to catch something floating out of his mind, then he shrugged dismissively. "No, it's gone. It can't have been important."

They found they were in between radio bulletins so Maltravers rang a friend of his at the Press Association news agency to see if they had heard anything about Luke Norman being found.

"Apparently not," he said as he replaced the receiver. "He said he'd check and call me back if there was anything but it doesn't appear likely or PA would know about it. Oliver must have told the police where they can find him if they need to. The fact he's been released doesn't necessarily mean they've finished with him."

"Well I'm going to see Joanna York," said Tess. "Wish me luck."

Joanna York was on the landing when the front-door bell rang. For a moment she leaned against the bannisters breathing deeply, then forced herself to go downstairs. Somehow she had to come to terms with what was happening to her, putting on a normal face to the rest of the world who must never be allowed to suspect the truth. She braced herself as she stood by the door then opened it, a smile stitched across her face with an effort.

"Hello again."

What was her name? She was the woman who had called earlier – the friend of that man Maltravers who had seen her in the square. Oh, please go away. Don't try to help. Nobody can help me.

"Look, I'm dreadfully sorry to be a nuisance, but could I possibly use your telephone? Peter and Susan's is on the blink and I've simply got to ring my agent in London. I don't know where the local phone boxes are and it will only take a moment."

Tess stood on the step, a smiling, unthreatening visitor asking a small favour. It was as if the incident outside the shop had never happened. Joanna York was so relieved that she appeared to have forgotten it and was treating her like a normal human being that it was as disorientating as sudden relief from pain. She had to stifle a gasp of pleasure.

"Of course, please come in. It's just by the door."

"That's awfully kind of you." Tess, all politeness, was looking for signs of what she had seen before. "It's only to London, it's a local call from here."

The front door opened straight into the tiny downstairs combined living and dining room with the stairs running up behind a wall in the corner. As Tess picked up the phone and dialled the number of her own flat, Joanna York went through into the kitchen extension on the back of the house. Tess played out a short rehearsed conversation with a ringing tone for a few moments, leaving the pauses at her end as brief as possible in case Joanna heard it, then hung up.

"Thank you. I must give you the money," she called through to the kitchen where she could see Joanna standing by the sink. "Have you any change?"

"It doesn't matter." Joanna York turned to her, picking up a tea towel to dry her hands. "It's only coppers . . . If you need it again, just ask."

Tess noticed the embarrassment and discomfort in the gesture that accompanied the offer, the hands nervously crumpling the towel, the smile artificial. In only a few hours Joanna York had gone from near total hysteria to apparent normality. Does not compute, thought Tess, and decided that a frontal attack might go straight through the slender defences.

"It seems all wrong worrying about silly things like business appointments at the moment, doesn't it?" She saw the flicker of apprehension in the girl's eyes. "It's so awful about Simon being murdered."

Oh, you poor kid, I've got you in one, she told herself as all the racking emotion she had seen earlier erupted back into the hesitant, nervous face. Joanna dropped her head very quickly, but too late to hide it. Tess crossed the small room and gently put her hand under her chin, lifting it like a child's.

"What *is* the matter?" she asked softly. "You don't know me and I don't know if I can help, but you are so unhappy aren't you?"

In certain states of mind, gentleness is a devastating and irresistible force and Joanna York crumpled under it. She threw her arms round a woman she hardly knew, her body convulsed with sobbing. Tess held her very firmly until the spasms subsided then led her to a chair by the large brick fireplace that filled half of one wall and made her sit down.

"Come on," she said coaxingly. "What is it?"

Joanna's breath stuttered for a few moments then she tried to speak but her voice was an inarticulate croak.

"Take your time," Tess said. "Hang on, I'll get some water."

She grabbed a cup from a wallrack in the kitchen and was filling it when she heard the front door open and Alister York came into the house. As Tess turned to see him, the figure of his wife flashed between them and there were frantic footsteps running up the stairs. Tess and York stared at each other as water overflowed from the cup she was still holding and gurgled down the drain.

"What are you doing here?" he asked stonily.

The water splashed on to Tess's hand and she put the cup down quickly and turned off the tap. The action gave her time to grasp the feeling that she should be very careful.

"I'd called to use your phone because Peter and Susan's is out of order," she said, turning back to face him. "Your wife seemed . . . unwell and I was just getting her some water."

York's eyes flashed upstairs and there was the wrong sort of concern in them.

"Well as I'm here now there's no need for you to be troubled any further," he said. "I'll take care of it."

His voice labelled Tess as an intruder in his house. As she hesitated, he stepped to one side, tacitly directing her out through the front door, still standing open behind him.

"If my wife is unwell, I must go to her. Will you please leave now?"

Tess could think of no arguments that she could possibly use to remain and York's look convinced her that it would be advisable to get away from him as quickly as possible.

"Of course." She crossed to the door warily, eyes never leaving his face as the distance between them diminished. "I hope she's soon better."

"I'm sure it's nothing serious," he replied.

The space between York and the wall was narrow and Tess paused fractionally in front of him, their eyes meeting at close range. She was instantly reminded of when she had been a drama student and Sir Ralph Richardson had frighteningly demonstrated how he conjured up evil with just the expression of his face; but the man she was looking at now was not acting. As York's burning eyes ordered her out, she felt scared of him.

Even before she was down the two shallow steps to the pavement outside, the door slammed behind her. She whirled round and looked at it helplessly for a moment then ran back up Bellringer Street like someone who has seen a child drowning and is unable to help. Inside the house, York put his briefcase on the table, picked up the telephone and dialled the Penroses' number; when Maltravers answered, York put the receiver down without a word then went upstairs. Her back and shoulders shuddering with crying, his wife was lying face downwards on the bed. "What did you tell her?" he asked quietly.

There was no reply, just a muffled sound from her mouth pressed against the bedclothes, a whimper for mercy. He took hold of her arm and savagely pulled her upright.

"What did you tell her?"

Joanna York's head shook mutely and helplessly, sobs and gasps choking out of her. York began to drag her like a doll across the room and she struggled violently in his grip before she fainted and lay crumpled at his feet.

Maltravers had just put down the telephone, dismissing the call as someone's ill-mannered response to dialling a wrong number, when Tess burst into the kitchen, face frozen, and ran straight past him into the dining room. When he followed her, she had opened the drinks cabinet and was agitatedly pouring herself a whisky, the decanter rattling against the rim of the glass. She crashed the decanter down and took half the drink at one swallow.

"What the hell has happened?" he demanded.

Stung by the shock of the alcohol, Tess shook her head violently as if to dispel terrible images. Maltravers crossed the room and put his hands on her shoulders.

"Tell me," he said firmly.

"I can't describe it. He came in just as I thought I was going to get her to talk. He . . ." She turned to Maltravers urgently. "Gus, he's mad! I know he is! We can't just leave her there with him, we've got to help!"

Maltravers looked at her for a moment. "You're not telling me. Come and sit down and start from the beginning."

They sat on adjacent chairs by the large circular oak dining table and he listened impassively as Tess pulled herself together and related everything that had happened.

133

"And what do you think?" he asked when she had finished.

Tess sat for a moment, looking at the glass cupped on her hands on the table, analysing and finding her conclusions.

"There's no other explanation. He must have killed Simon," she said finally. "We're right, I'm positive we are . . . Christ, it's like waking up in a Hammer movie. Give me a cigarette."

"You've given up."

"I've just started again. This is worse than the risk of cancer."

She was still embroiled in her thoughts as she dipped the end of the cigarette into the flame of Maltravers' lighter, drew deeply then blew out the smoke with a grimace of revulsion.

"God, it tastes awful." She took another mouthful of whisky. "That's better. Gus, we've got to tell the police what's happening."

Maltravers leaned back in his chair and regarded her gravely.

"And what do we tell them?" he asked. "We've still got nothing more than an hysterical woman, a domineering husband and an unprovable guess. No . . ." He held up his hand to prevent Tess's protests. "We don't have a single, solid fact and it's very likely that your visit may have put her into a state where she won't talk to anybody, including the police. At the moment they have two leading suspects and are not likely to be interested in theories without hard evidence to support them. Believe me, I feel as badly about this as you do, but the police do not take kindly to people shouting bloody murder from the housetops because of a half-baked idea. We need proof."

"And how do we find it?" Tess looked at him pleadingly. "Because I'm sure we have got to.".

Maltravers sighed. "I don't know. I wish to God I did. Perhaps if the police could get Oliver and Luke Norman out of the way, then they might – "

The telephone rang in the kitchen. When Maltravers answered, it was his contact at PA calling back.

"Where do you get your tips from, then? We've just got reports coming in that there have been two sightings of Luke Norman driving towards Penzance."

"How definite are they?" Maltravers asked.

"The police are apparently taking them seriously enough to have half the force in Cornwall looking for him. At least that's what the local stringer tells us and he's reliable enough. We're just putting out a wireservice rush on it."

Maltravers mentally visualised the dwindling triangle of the county where England tapered off into the sea; if Norman was beyond Penzance there were very few ways out.

"If it's true, they won't need many road blocks to catch him then," he commented. "Thanks for calling back. I owe you a drink."

Absently swirling the last half-inch of whisky around in the bottom of her glass, Tess looked drawn and worried as Maltravers returned to the sitting room.

"It looks as though the police may be closing in on Luke Norman and it may not take them very long to catch him." He explained what he had just been told. "I think that for the time being we may have to leave Joanna York alone. If they find Luke and it turns out that he killed Simon, then whatever's happening down the hill may be totally unconnected. There appears to be something very wrong there, but we don't know what it is – and can we make it our business if it's nothing to do with the murder? At the moment we can really only wait and see what happens. All right?"

Tess's abstracted nod was only token agreement. She was convinced that a few minutes earlier she had stood face to face with Simon's killer and that there had to be some other explanation for Luke Norman running away.

"No, it's not all right," she said. "And you know it isn't. I just hope to God that Bellringer Street doesn't end up with another murder on its doorstep because everyone's running round in circles looking for the wrong man."

Chapter Ten

Stars blinked and twinkled in an ink-black sky and the sea was black, dancing silver, licking gently against the rocks at the foot of the cliffs a hundred feet below where Luke Norman sat on the narrow, grassy path between Lamorna and Porthcurno. Exhausted, drained of fear and panic, he stared at the jagged, shining blade laid across the water by the moon, his mind filled now only with regret and remembered love. He had been there for nearly five hours after leaving his car and walking along the coast path until he had suddenly decided to stop and try to think. In the whispering darkness he watched a fishing boat slowly cross the light-path of the moon, reliving another warm night in Greece when he had first met Simon. He lowered his head on his knee and started to rock slowly backwards and forwards as he wept.

The police were within a hundred and fifty yards of him when he heard them, a crackling voice on a radio carrying through the silence. He looked to his left in terror and saw two torchlight beams, glow-worm flickers like sparks creeping along burnt wood. There was nothing visible to his right. Cautiously he stood up and moved away, half crouching, invisible against the deep grey headland rising behind him. The path was rough and twice his foot slipped as he climbed upwards, stumbling against small boulders in the twilight. After about a quarter of a mile, the path divided and he hesitated, looking back to see the quivering torchlights edging closer, before taking the way downwards. As the police reached the high point behind him, they saw the silhouette of his moving figure against the polished backdrop of the sea where the land dropped away beyond, and shouted.

Luke Norman began to run wildly and suddenly there was loose, sliding scree beneath his feet. He fell clumsily face downwards, grabbing at the short coarse grass, his feet scrabbling for firm ground. They found it and he pushed himself upwards with his hands just as his foothold betrayed him, his weight wrenching a small rock out of the earth. His arms swung crazily as he fought to regain his balance then he toppled backwards, his head striking another stone, half stunning him as he rolled down the steep slope towards the pewter mirror of the sea. A chatter of small pebbles gathered as they slid down with him until they began to tumble over the cliff edge. Luke Norman fell among them and they rattled off the barbed surfaces of the huge pointed rock sticking up like a crude arrowhead that split his body open. He died during the half-hour it took the police to climb down and find him.

The story broke too late for the morning papers but Maltravers and Peter heard it on Breakfast Time television while Tess was taking the children to school. Self-conscious of the presence of the cameras, a customer from the curiously named Lamorna Wink pub told how he had walked down to the cove after closing time to gain brief and meaningless fame as the man who discovered Luke Norman's car. The picture changed to library film shot from a plane flying along the rough-torn edges of the Cornish coast.

"Police recovered the body from the rocks on a small inlet about half a mile from the popular holiday beach at Porthcurno," the commentary reported. "Officers from Capley are expected here later this morning. At this stage, the police are treating the death as accidental. A spokesman said that Mr Norman appeared to fall off the narrow, treacherous path as he was trying to run away."

The screen blinked again to show a reporter standing in front of Penzance police station.

"Luke Norman was wanted for questioning in connection with the murder at the weekend of Lord Dunford, the heir to Lord Pembury of Edenbridge House. After the murder . . ."

"So where does that leave everyone?" Maltravers asked as he turned away from the set. He and Tess had decided not to share their suspicions about York with anyone until they had something solid to go on.

"With a murderer, presumably," said Peter. "Nothing else makes sense."

"But where's the actual proof?" Maltravers argued. "Luke Norman could have been over-distressed at Simon's death and terrified that he was a major suspect. All that's happened could have been the result of blind panic. There's no way the police are going to wrap it all up yet. It still could have been Oliver. I'd like to know how the police are treating it, but I can't see any way we can find out at the moment."

"I know somebody who'll be able to tell us," said Peter.

"Who?"

"Harry Matthews on the *Capley Citizen*. He's an idle bugger of the old school but he's got marvellous police contacts and they tell him all sorts of things off the record. He owes me a favour for tipping him off about a bank raid in the New Town." Peter glanced at the clock. "Can't try for a while though. Harry thinks it's indecent to arrive for work before half past ten. Better still, he's always in the office pub at lunchtime. I'll try him there on my way to see Susan. Come with me if you want. It's quite an experience meeting Harry."

Keith Miller received the report from the officers he had sent to Penzance gloomily. There was no question but that the body was that of Luke Norman and would have to remain in Cornwall until the inquest had been held. Norman's car had not contained either of the missing cricket balls, Dunford's tie or a convenient note of confession. Miller tossed the message back on to his desk in irritation.

"Fuck it," he said unemotionally to Parry. "I needed this like a sick headache. I'm even more convinced now it was him, but how do we prove it? He could have tossed a cricket ball away anywhere between here and the West Country. We can't search the whole sodding M4."

"And the M5," Parry added. Miller scowled at him. "But he might not have done that, Sir. He could have dumped it when he ran off from the house."

"All right, but where? We've done everything in that churchyard except dig up the graves and there's no sign of either of the damned things there or in the Darbys' garden."

"His car was parked at Edenbridge House," Parry pointed out. "He could have chucked it somewhere in the park as he drove off."

Miller pulled a face, contemplating the wide spaces of Edenbridge Park which Norman could have driven through as he escaped from Old Capley.

"All right," he said resignedly. "I'll try and get more men and you see how many reliable civilians you can round up to help. God, it could take weeks – and even then it might not prove anything."

"There's still Hawkhurst," Parry added and Miller noted the hopeful tone of his voice.

"Yes," he agreed. "But it's much the same position isn't it? Proof, Sergeant, we need some bloody proof, *any* bloody proof and we need it in a hurry. The Chief Constable is not best pleased at the moment. The most notorious murder that this force has had to deal with for fifty years is playing havoc with his ulcer and he wants results. Oh, get on with it."

After Parry left, Miller made a series of phone calls to senior officers in both his own and neighbouring county forces and managed to collect another twenty men. Then he picked up the report from Penzance again, read it sourly and once again regretted that his annual leave had not started a week earlier. All his instincts were telling him that Luke Norman was his man. Everything – motive, opportunity, his escape from the scene, his fatal running away in the night when the police reached him – every aspect pointed in that direction. Had they caught Norman, Miller was sure he would have confessed; now he was a body on a mortuary slab with his secret. Hawkhurst? Miller shook his head impatiently. Too obvious . . . and yet the alibi he had offered had fallen apart at the first touch. York? A tiny muscle in Miller's left cheek twitched slightly, which often happened when his brain was trying to tell him something.

Oliver Hawkhurst heard the news about Luke Norman with much less dissatisfaction than Miller. The police suspicion of his cousin's lover had taken a great deal of pressure off him and, being a latent queer-basher among his other unlovely habits, the prospect of Norman being jailed for life had appealed to him. As far as Hawkhurst was concerned, Norman must still be the obvious suspect – and now could it ever be proved that he *didn't* do it? As he drove to Edenbridge House for a meeting with Lord Pembury and Sir Gerald, he wondered what the police did in such circumstances. Unless something else came to light, they presumably lost interest in the matter after sufficient time had elapsed. Not a completely satisfactory position from Hawkhurst's point of view, but better than the alternatives. The immediate question was, where did it leave him in relation to inheriting Edenbridge? The meeting with his uncle and his lawyer should clarify that. As the butler led him along the corridor to the study, Hawkhurst adjusted his newly-bought black tie and composed his face into an appearance of suitable solemnity and regret.

"Ah, Oliver," Pembury said as he was let into the room. "I don't think you know Sir Gerald."

"No, but I know Sir Gerald's reputation." As Piers-Freeman acknowledged with a gracious smile, Hawkhurst congratulated himself on a good start. He sat down opposite Pembury and looked across the desk expectantly. When he left Edenbridge House two hours later he was furious and would happily have strangled both Lord Pembury and his lawyer.

Sir Gerald had at first been apologetic. It was to be deplored that Mr Hawkhurst should remain the subject of police inquiries. Clearly some confirmation that Luke Norman had been the murderer was greatly to be desired. However – Sir Gerald had gestured elegantly – for the time being, his advice must be that it would not be correct for Mr Hawkhurst to be officially recognised as the heir. Doubtless this most unsatisfactory situation would eventually resolve itself, but . . . Mr Hawkhurst understood? Oliver Hawkhurst found it intolerable, but remained silent.

Then Lord Pembury had spoken. He accepted the legal advice, but saw no reason for not acquainting his nephew with certain facts about the ownership of Edenbridge which he felt sure would eventually devolve to him. Hawkhurst controlled his sense of elation, a feat which became increasingly easy as Pembury outlined the incredibly strict controls that would be placed on him by the Edenbridge Trustees. As far as he could make out, he would not be able to go out and buy a newspaper without first obtaining their permission. Quite simply, Edenbridge was locked for all time in a legal straitjacket and all future holders of the title would in effect be tenants in their own ancestral home. A junior accountant with a firm in London would have more power over the Pembury wealth than Oliver would ever have – if it ever became his. For all the good that Dunford's death had done him, he might as well have lived.

Oliver Hawkhurst had not recognised that very old money was kept in very strong boxes and other people held the keys. Lord Pembury had never thought that his nephew was very bright and found their direct blood connection rather unfortunate. But he was the only possible heir – unless he turned out to be a murderer, a prospect Lord Pembury did not choose to consider.

Harry Matthews flopped against the bar with the elegance of a beached walrus. He looked as though he had slept in his suit and would need to check his diary to see when he had last changed his shirt. His hair had settled around the back of his head with a few strands stubbornly remaining in the centre of his forehead, swept back across his crown like fine pencil lines. The pint glass looked minute in his massive paw of a hand and Maltravers watched in admiration as more than three quarters of its contents disappeared into his mouth almost as swiftly as they could have been poured into a bucket. There was a legend on the *Capley Citizen* that when Harry had once gone on the wagon for a month, the biggest brewery in the county had been forced to lay off the night shift.

"Thanks, Peter," Matthews grunted. "Needed that." He burped resonantly and removed the froth from his thick, lank moustache with a downward movement of his hand, as though squeezing any escaping drops of beer on to his upper lip. "Anyway, what brings you in here? Thought you only drank with the nobs in the Old Town."

"We'd like a bit of information, Harry," Peter said. "Incidentally, this is Gus Maltravers, a friend of mine."

Matthews made some indecipherable sound of greeting then turned back to Peter. "Information about what?"

"Whatever the police are saying off the record about this Luke Norman business. Do they still think he killed Dunford?"

Matthews sucked in his breath through blubbery lips, making a noise like a child dragging the last drops of a drink up through a straw. Maltravers sensed that information would require more lubrication before it started to flow.

"Another pint?" he suggested. "You've done considerable damage to that one." The speed with which Matthews finished his drink and pushed the glass across to the barmaid was incredible in a man who looked as though he would even sneeze in slow motion.

"Same again, Betty," he said, then glanced at Peter again. "So what do you want to know?"

"Anything you can tell us. You must have been checking it out this morning."

"Had a chat with a couple of contacts," Matthews admitted. "Not much I can tell you though. There's nothing to prove Norman did it and Keith Miller's ordered a search of the park for the cricket balls. The medical evidence proves that's what was used to kill him. That's about it."

"But is he still the chief suspect?" Maltravers pressed.

"He is as far as Miller's concerned. Dave Parry says he still thinks it could have been Dunford's cousin but they've released him for the time being."

"And there's nobody else?"

Matthews looked at Maltravers sharply as he put the question. Somewhere inside the overweight ruin of a journalist, idling out the end of his career with the barest minimum of effort, were the rusting remains of a first-class reporter.

"Should there be?"

"I don't know," said Maltravers. "I thought you might."

Matthews turned off again when he realised he was not about to be given a tip without having to make any particular effort.

"Not that I've heard of," he said. "And I'd have heard. Let's have a couple of those meat pies, Betty. What about you gents?"

They remained with Matthews for an hour during which he did not buy a single drink although the occasion later appeared on his expenses as a meeting with two local councillors and cost his editor seven pounds. Maltravers found the burned-out newspaperman, who had let his talent rot in the provinces because he lacked the ambition to climb higher, entertaining company. If he ever decided to use only half his ability and experience he would leave the brash young Turks on the *Capley Citizen* for dead. And his contacts in the police, among them senior officers with whom he had drunk as raw, beat bobbies, were impeccable. By the time they left, Maltravers was sure he

could have found out no more about the inquiry into Dunford's murder if the police had offered him the freedom of the
incident room.

"He's one of a dying breed, isn't he?" he remarked as Peter
drove him back into Old Capley before going on to visit Susan
and the baby. "And I admire his local knowledge, even if it
doesn't tell us very much. How big is Edenbridge Park?"

"I'm not sure," said Peter. "Several hundred acres."

"Possibly containing one cricket ball that . . . Just a
minute . . . There could be dozens of lost cricket balls out
there . . . I nearly hooked a couple across that short leg side
boundary."

"Believe it or not, I've done it myself," said Peter. "The
local kids turn them up long after a match – and usually keep
them."

"Which means that if Luke threw the ball away somewhere
near the cricket pitch, somebody could already have found it
and it could be anywhere by now," said Maltravers, thinking
through new possibilities. "Would he have driven near there
on his way out?"

"He could have done. There are several ways in and out of
the park, but as far as I know only two gates are left open all
night. If he used the main gates he would have driven right
past the pitch, or he could have gone out through East Sutton,
which is a hamlet right over the far side of the park. Luke
could know about it from previous visits and it's a more
private exit than the main entrance."

"How far is it from the house?"

"To East Sutton?" Peter mentally calculated for a moment.
"Certainly more than a mile, possibly a mile and a half. Then
it's country lanes for another couple of miles until you reach
the A1 into London."

"That's an awful lot of country to lose any number of cricket
balls in," Maltravers observed. "I don't envy the police the
search. But that's where the murder weapon could be."

"And what about the second cricket ball?" Peter queried. "And the tie?"

"Among life's little mysteries," said Maltravers.

Tess had driven into London after dropping the children off at school to buy a present for Susan's baby – one look at the New Town shops had convinced her she would find nothing she liked there – and was still not back when Maltravers returned to Bellringer Street. He noticed that the police had disappeared from the churchyard and decided to walk round and see if he could find Susannah's grave among the ancient dead of the parish. Its obscurity meant that it took him nearly half an hour of bending down to read faded inscriptions, including one to a woman who had buried seven children before mercifully joining them herself. As he was standing by the lonely stone to the unhappy daughter that the Pembury family had ruthlessly cast out of their lives, he saw Joanna York walking in through the church gates, her arms filled with Enchantment lilies and carnations. He was sure that she had noticed him because she hesitated for the briefest moment before walking quickly on and disappearing into the church. After a few minutes he followed her.

There was no sign of her at first, then he spotted her arranging the flowers in a vase near the altar. He dropped some coins in a box by the door and helped himself to a pamphlet on the church's history before casually making his way down the aisle, apparently looking for various features to which visitors' attention was drawn. It was impossible to move completely quietly in the hollow vault of the building, but he noticed that she never turned round to see who had come in and he had almost reached her before he spoke.

"Good afternoon. It's Mrs York, isn't it?"

"What?" She turned as if startled that someone had crept up on her. "Oh, Mr . . . Maltravers. What are you doing here?"

"Playing at tourists." He waved the pamphlet as evidence then indicated the vase. "Do you always do this?"

"Pardon? Oh, the flowers. There's a rota and it's my turn this week. We put fresh ones in the church nearly every day."

"How nice." Maltravers smiled. "Can you tell me . . . I've just been reading about the Pembury chapel, but I'm not sure where it is. Is it open to the public?"

"Oh, yes . . . it's over there." She gestured to her left. "Anybody can go in."

"Thank you. You see, I remember you were telling me about the history of Old Capley. At the party. You were saying something about . . . which Earl was it? The second? The one who was the father of Tom Bostock the highwayman."

Something flickered through her eyes and she looked away. "No, the third."

Maltravers felt like a fencer, circling an opponent, gingerly probing for an opening.

"Of course, I should have remembered . . . I presume he's buried there?"

"Yes." She turned back to the flowers.

"Thank you. This way you said?" Maltravers moved a few paces away but kept his eyes on her visibly nervous back.

"How tragic that the next man to be put there should be so young," he added. "You must have known Lord Dunford quite well, with your husband working at the house . . . Did you know him quite well, Mrs York?"

Joanna York froze, holding a long-stemmed, ghost-white lily at the lip of the vase, and there was a very long silence. Maltravers waited, then, without warning, she turned and ran down the aisle, the sound of her flat shoes on the stone floor of the nave slapping round the walls.

"*Joanna!*" Maltravers shouted after her, and his voice was amplified by the stones so that it hammered through the entire, silent building like a booming gong. "What's the matter? I want to help you!"

The door at the far end of the church slammed and the impact crashed through St Barbara's swamping the fading

146

echoes of Maltravers' shout then died away itself to leave an icy hush.

"If you prick us, do we not . . . scream?" Maltravers murmured.

At the church door he picked up the lily which Joanna York had dropped as she ran away, its stem twisted and crushed as though it had been squeezed very hard in the hand. He was carrying it as he entered the Penroses' house and found that Tess had returned.

"Been stealing flowers?" she asked. "Or aren't I worth a whole bunch?"

"It's from the church," said Maltravers. "I've just had another encounter with Joanna York and it only took one gentle push from me for her to fall over."

He laid the lily on the table. "I don't know what's festering there, but it stinks more than these ever would. Incidentally, the police still think it was Luke."

That evening Maltravers peered at Susan's baby sleeping in the perspex cot beside her bed in the maternity ward.

"'Golden the light on the locks of Myfanwy, Golden the light on the book on her knee,'" he intoned. "'Finger-marked pages of Rackham's Hans Andersen, Time for the children to come down to tea.'"

"Gus, what on earth are you doing?" Susan demanded.

"Anything I say to him at this stage will be gibberish," he replied. "So it may as well be first-rate gibberish. With a little luck, some of it may sink in. There will be no 'Diddums then?' from Uncle Gus."

"Idiot. We are still going to call him after you," Susan said. "If it had been a girl, she'd have been called Tess. You two have been marvellous."

"I'll sympathise with you when you're older," Maltravers told his namesake. "Just be grateful that my father didn't let his passion for Gibbon saddle us both with Tiberius or Caligula.

147

Good night, sweet prince, and flights of angels sing thee to thy rest."

He sat on the edge of the bed and listened to an incomprehensible conversation between Tess and Susan relating to the feeding and general maintenance of the very young. Tess had said as they drove to the hospital that she intended raising the question of Joanna York with Susan – without telling her everything – but the infant Augustus took priority. Finally Tess edged towards the subject, underplaying her concern.

"It may not be important, but we've had . . . what is it? . . . three instances now where she seemed to be terribly upset about something," she said. "We're wondering if it might help if she talked to somebody, but we don't know who the best person might be. Has she any particular friends who could help?"

"Joanna's on everyone's fringes," Susan replied. "Not having children means she doesn't share a lot of things with the rest of us and she's very shy as well. And Alister keeps her on such a tight rein that I sometimes think she has to ask his permission to get out of the house. If she's with a group of the girls, she just sits there mumchance while the rest of us are rabbiting on. Everybody likes her, but, frankly, we get impatient with her. I don't think she has any real friends, just people she knows."

"But women always make friends," Tess objected. "They're better at it than men."

"Not Joanna," Susan insisted. "I think that Alister sees to that."

Maltravers jumped in alarm as the baby woke beside him with a tiny cry.

"Dinnertime," said Susan. "Pass him over, Gus. Don't worry, he won't bite."

Maltravers gingerly pulled back the openweave blanket like a bomb disposal expert on a trying day and looked hesitantly at what appeared to be an impossibly small and fragile body.

"Just hold him firmly," Susan instructed. "You're a lovely man, but God, you're helpless."

Apprehensively, Maltravers closed his hands around the baby and lifted him up, trying to calculate the balance between holding firmly and squeezing to death, and offered Susan her son as if presenting her with a cup she had won.

"There, that wasn't so bad was it?" she said. "You'll be better when you have some of your own. You can stay if you want, but this will take a while."

Slickly and expertly, Susan cradled her son in one arm and started to pull the top of her nightgown open.

"I'll take Gus away." Tess stood up and started to close the curtains around the bed. "Natural functions trouble him. We'll see you again before we go."

"When are you leaving?"

"In a couple of days. You'll be home then and you certainly don't want us cluttering up the place. We'll come back for the christening."

Susan reached out with her free arm and took hold of Tess's hand. "No speeches, just thank you. Sorry it's been such a rotten visit."

"Forget it." Tess leaned down and kissed her. "Just look after yourself, you hear. We'll be in touch."

Maltravers instinctively felt that Peter and Susan's very personal problems, brutally torn open by Dunford's murder, were showing distinct signs of repair. He winked at her as he lowered his head and kissed her; out of the little raver in the accounts department all those years ago, a very strong lady had emerged.

"Thank God it wasn't Simon's baby," Tess said as they walked down the hospital corridor. "She couldn't have stood that."

"I bow to the mysterious knowledge of women in such matters," said Maltravers. "Actually, I thought the one in the next cot looked exactly the same. But we're no further forward with the Joanna York matter."

"No," Tess said resignedly. "It worries me sick that we might have to just walk away from it."

149

The limited parking space in Bellringer Street was occupied by residents, visitors and pub customers when they returned and Maltravers could only find a space for his car near the bottom of the hill. As they walked up past the Batsman, they reached the Yorks' house and instinctively glanced in through the front window. Alister York was sitting at the table just inside and looked straight back at them, his face hardening when he recognised Tess. Caught off guard, the thoughts that obsessed her remained on her face for a fraction of a second before she switched on a glassy smile and walked on. York remained staring out of the window across the empty street at the corner of the Darbys' house opposite and a look of vivid loathing seeped across his features. A few yards up the street, Tess shuddered as she took Maltravers' arm and held it very tightly.

Chapter Eleven

Damp, fat, biscuit-coloured mushrooms plopped into the shallow wooden trug basket as Mrs Sarah Hickson meandered through Edenbridge Park, the sheen of dew staining stout sensible shoes. The park would not be open to the public for another three hours, but Mrs Hickson knew the Bellringer Street gatekeeper and was allowed a special dispensation to go in early whenever she wished. And while collecting her breakfast in the shimmering, moist morning she found the cricket ball that had killed Dunford.

Mrs Hickson was an extremely private person, living a retired, almost reclusive existence centred on the church, memories of her late husband and a succession of Burmese cats. Convinced, like the late Lord Pembury, that the world had become a violent and tasteless place, she had as little to do with it as possible. She rarely watched, read or listened to the news and, if she did, she would shake her head sorrowfully and dismiss such awful things from her gentle mind. Although nearly eighty, she was small, sprightly and independent, polite to her neighbours but never happier than when she was alone in her small house next door to the Penroses, surrounded by the souvenirs of her life and minding her own business. She did not know certain things because she did not wish to know them. She had heard about the murder with great shock, but had then rejected it as something unpleasant, so she was the only person in Old Capley who was unaware that the police were looking for a cricket ball. Even seeing them search in the churchyard as she walked back up Bellringer Street from the shops had not excited her curiosity, because she had no curiosity. She picked the ball up and laid it carefully to one side of the mushrooms before making her way out of the park and going home. At that time in the morning, there was no one about to see her. Fortunately she liked young Timothy next door, whom she regarded as a very well brought-up little boy.

It was ten o'clock when the front door bell rang and Maltravers answered.

"Is Mrs Penrose in?" asked Mrs Hickson.

"I'm afraid not . . . she's had a baby you know."

"Really? I didn't know." Maltravers realised from the reply that the little bird-like lady on the step was certainly not the local gossip. "However," she continued. "All I wanted was to give her this. I know that young Timothy enjoys a game of cricket. It's a bit dirty, but I'm sure it can be cleaned."

Maltravers stood very still indeed as she held out her hand towards him. It was not dirt sticking to the ball she was holding; it looked very much like strands of hair stuck in some deeper red than the leather surface.

"Where did you find that?" he asked cautiously.

"Oh, in the park. You often come across them near the cricket pitch. I usually leave them with the gatekeeper but he wasn't about this morning and I don't think the cricket club will miss just one, will they? It seems quite old but Timothy can use it."

Maltravers stepped back slightly.

"Would you come in for a moment, please?"

Mrs Hickson looked reluctant. "No, I'll just leave it . . ." She jumped as Maltravers reached forward, took hold of her arm and dragged her into the house. "Let go of me, young man! What do you think – ?"

"Come in," he interrupted firmly, steering her into the kitchen where Tess looked up enquiringly from the washing up of a late breakfast. "It's quite all right, but there are a number of things you really ought to know. I'll take that, thank you."

To Mrs Hickson's consternation, he grabbed hold of a kitchen towel and very carefully took the cricket ball out of her hand.

"This lady is Miss Davy who will explain everything," he said. "I've got to make a phone call. Darling, this lady's found the bloody thing." Mrs Hickson looked offended; bad language on top of abduction. As he dialled the number of Capley police station, Maltravers was staggered by the element of farce in it all.

By the time the police arrived a few minutes later, Tess had managed to reassure Mrs Hickson that she had not fallen into the clutches of a maniac but that she had become an unsuspecting part of a murder inquiry.

"Did you really not know the police were looking for a cricket ball?" Tess asked in disbelief. "It was the murder weapon."

"I did not." Mrs Hickson appeared to find the question faintly offensive. "We don't all pry into other people's business."

Maltravers and Tess looked at each other helplessly, unable to think of any adequate response.

One policeman took Mrs Hickson back to her cottage for a statement while another placed the ball in a plastic bag and drove back to Capley police station, warning both Maltravers and Tess that statements might also be required from them. After they had all left, Maltravers rang Peter at his office.

"Old Sally Hickson found it?" Peter roared with disbelieving laughter. "God, she could have kept it for weeks and never thought about it. It's lucky she didn't throw it away. Are you sure it's the right one?"

"I could see what looked like human hair and dried blood on it," Maltravers told him. "The question is, are there finger-prints? And whose are they? I think we need Harry Matthews again."

"I'll call him," said Peter. "I'll tip him off that the ball's been found on condition that he lets me know the results when somebody tells him. It's press day on the *Citizen* so he should be very grateful for a front-page lead handed him on a plate. Call you when I hear anything back."

Maltravers put the phone down and stared at the wall thoughtfully for a moment before turning to Tess.

"It looks as though we'll know – at least unofficially – fairly soon," he said. "But you realise what all this means, don't you? Mrs Hickson told us she found the ball on the far side of the cricket pitch, about a quarter of a mile from the house. Harry Matthews said Oliver's story is that he went straight from the party to spend the rest of the night with some woman in Bellringer Street and then he was picked up by the police at Edenbridge House. If that's true, he can't have put it there. And there's no way that York could have. He found Simon's body and would have been searched like the rest of us before he left the Darbys'. I know he's a cricketer and a strong man, but he can't have leaned out of that study window just across the road and thrown it – what? – perhaps half a mile right into the park. It's *got* to have been Luke."

Tess paused for a moment, then shook her head impatiently.

"But York could be lying about coming straight downstairs after he found Simon's body," she argued. "He could have left the house first, thrown away the ball and then come back. Couldn't he?"

"Darling, you're grasping at straws and you know it," Maltravers told her. "What sort of sense does that make? There's no way he would have left the body hoping nobody would find it while he went into the park and dropped the ball in the grass – and surely he'd have found a better place to hide it than that – and came back to the house. Why would he do such a thing? We've got to accept that everything is pointing to Luke at the moment, and if that's the case Joanna's behaviour presumably has nothing to do with the murder."

But as Tess failed to find flaws in Maltravers' logic, he had the nagging feeling that he was missing the significance of something he had just said.

There was no call back from Peter with news from Harry Matthews for the rest of the morning and Maltravers left the

Ansaphone connected while they went to the Batsman for lunch again. It seemed that nobody in the bar had heard of Mrs Hickson's discovery and Dunford's murder had been replaced as a general topic of conversation by discussion of the finely balanced test match at Trent Bridge that was to end that day. Even without any confirming evidence, Luke Norman's running away and death – suspected by some not to have been accidental but deliberate – had settled the matter as far as most people were concerned. Maltravers and Tess sat in a corner of the bar, quietly going over what they knew.

"When do you think this Matthews man will call?" Tess asked.

"It could be any time. First of all he's got to get his contacts to talk – although that won't take him long – then he's got to catch his deadline," said Maltravers. "He'll let Peter know all right, but I rather suspect that he'll make himself a bit of money by tipping off the nationals first."

"Well, I'm not staying in all afternoon waiting," said Tess. "If there's nothing from Peter when we get back, let's leave the Ansaphone on and go for a walk in the park."

Maltravers looked offended. "Darling, England are more than a hundred behind with four wickets left. The final session's on television this afternoon."

Tess looked at him crossly. "This bloody visit started with cricket and now it's going to end with it? Oh, all right, if it's that important. I expect there's nothing else to do – but you watch it on your own and don't tell me all about it afterwards. And, incidentally, I shall expect a very good dinner out when we get back to town." She paused and smiled wickedly. "Langan's I think. And I mean the Brasserie. And I mean downstairs."

Maltravers flinched. Downstairs at Langan's was for international superstars and others of the very rich and his previous visit there with Tess was still appearing on his credit card demands.

"All right," he agreed reluctantly. "But it counts as a treat for your next three birthdays."

As they were eating, Alister York was sitting in his office in Edenbridge House, his mind obsessed with the image of Tess Davy. He had dismissed the possibility that Maltravers' answering the Penroses' phone had meant it had only been taking incoming calls; the woman had simply lied in order to get into his own house and talk to his wife. Joanna had repeated insistently that she had told her nothing, but York did not completely believe her. The Davy woman could only have come to the house because she suspected something was happening – God only knew how – and would she leave it alone? If Joanna had even hinted . . . Once again Alister York returned to the relentless conviction that the woman's interference threatened him with exposure. And exposure was unthinkable.

His chair squeaked as he spun it round and looked out of his window through which he could see the Bellringer Street gate of the park in the distance. Just beyond that gate was the house where Tess Davy was staying and it was as if his narrowed eyes were trying to pierce the solid brickwork to see her and read her thoughts. As he concentrated, tense with gathering anger, his thick-muscled right hand unconsciously closed around an apple he had taken for his lunch. There was a sudden squelching sound as it split under the pressure and his fingers were covered with crushed pulp.

There was no message from Peter when they returned and Maltravers stretched himself out in front of the television in the upstairs sitting room just as the England batsmen were walking out. Tess actually watched for a few minutes during which absolutely nothing seemed to happen, then gave up in despair.

"See you later," she said. "Peter told me of a longish walk that avoids the tourists so I may be a while. I hope they score lots of goals. 'Bye."

Maltravers grunted, already too absorbed to notice Tess's parting sideswipe, and she walked out of the house and up Bellringer Street alone. From his office window, York saw her enter the park and immediately turn right along the old stagecoach road from London that now wound almost deserted through the farmlands that lay about the house. It was an area used by very few people, leading to small lanes between the fields. As she vanished out of his sight, sand-shower of hair bouncing above her slender figure, he began to think again as unexpected opportunity danced before him.

"Good shot," Maltravers murmured as an England batsman glanced the ball between slips and gulley, wielding his bat as delicately as a fly-fisherman. Achieving ninety-two more runs engrossed him totally for another twenty minutes before somebody attempted a dangerous single and was left hopelessly stranded between the wickets as a fielder hurled the ball in from deep extra cover to run him out. Maltravers cursed and watched the replay, grudgingly admiring the accuracy of the fielder's throw. He remembered the similar effort by Alister York during the Town v. Estate match and two things suddenly made a ridiculous connection in his mind. He frowned at the suggestion for a moment, then stood up and opened the window, looking first across and slightly to his right down Bellringer Street at the Darbys' house, then leaning out to confirm that York lived almost opposite. So it could have been done, but what sense did it make? He straightened up, staring at the tower of St Barbara's facing him, like someone trying to imagine a complete picture from a fragment. Why did the dead butler in the Pembury chapel keep coming back, insisting there was something important there? He went over the curious story Tess had told him but could see nothing. Then he remembered saying something about it being a very odd skeleton in . . .

"Dear God!" he said aloud. "That can't be true!" Within a few minutes he had persuaded himself that it could and his face went very cold.

All that Tess could hear was scattered birdsong, the crisp throb of crickets and the susurration of growing things; the ceaseless technological clamour of the twentieth century from an endless variety of engines had completely faded. Such moments were rare in the densely populated area of the Home Counties and she stood in the pavilion of sky and sunshine that seemed to brim over the edges of Edenbridge Park, rejoicing in it. It lasted for about thirty seconds before the drone of an aeroplane crept distantly in from one corner. She smiled ruefully and moved on, grateful for the fleeting benison of quietness. Less than a mile from where she was walking, Edenbridge House was surrounded by visitors and their commotion; few would wander far from the area immediately adjacent to the house and discover the peace and solitude of the rest of the park.

She reached a point where a lane branched off at right angles from the road and paused. Peter had told her that the turning offered a route through some of the most unspoilt areas of the Edenbridge estate and a challenging set of stepping stones across a stream in the woods. She was starting to feel hot and the promised shade of trees was attractive. She passed first between high hawthorn hedges that gave on to parallel low wooden fences on either side, one stretch restricting the nomadic instincts of a herd of cows. The lane curved slightly to the left and for another blessed moment the silence came again. She leaned against the fence soaking in the calm tranquillity after the traumas of death, birth and mystery. She remembered Simon, his gallantry and his confusion and the terrible thought of his dead body. Luke Norman she had hardly spoken to but had instinctively liked; could he really have killed the man he loved? Then the image of Joanna York's horror-graven face came back, merging in and out with the cruel stare of her husband. Tess looked down at the long stem of grass she had plucked, idly splitting it with her thumbnail. What was that man doing to her? What had that man done? As she wrestled with it, she heard the sound of a car approaching along the lane where she had just walked, still invisible round the bend.

Tess was satisfied there was space for the vehicle to pass as it appeared in her view and she heard the gears drop. There was a vicious roar as the accelerator was slammed down and the vehicle leapt forward. Tess's annoyance at the stupidity of anyone driving so fast in such circumstances was instantly transmuted into the realisation that there was something wrong. There had to be a reason for such a senseless action and she abruptly knew what it was; the driver was going to run her down deliberately.

She neither froze nor screamed. Boosted by an internal torrent of adrenalin, she somersaulted over the fence, half propelled by the rush of air as the car swept past terrifyingly close. She bumped her head as she landed then rolled, slightly dazed, for several feet, breath pounded out of her lungs. A nearby cow lumbered clumsily and hastily away. As she lay on the ground, inconsequentially reflecting that acting is a profession that keeps you fit, she heard the screech of brakes. Still winded, she heard a car door open and someone climb over the fence then a man appeared above her, head a gold-haloed silhouette against the brilliant sun. She tried to look up at him, but her eyes crinkled against the brightness.

"Miss Davy! Are you all right?" The voice somehow sounded as if he would prefer that she was not.

"No thanks to you!" she gasped. "You nearly killed me!"

"It would have been an accident. I didn't expect there to be anybody on this road. Here, let me help you up."

Fear overcame physical discomfort as Alister York leaned forward, large menacing hand extended. Tess scrambled to her feet and stepped back several paces.

"Don't you touch me!" she shouted. "I am going straight to the police about this and I'll *make* them listen to me! You tried to kill me because I've been talking to your wife didn't you?"

"And why should I be bothered about that?" he asked softly.

"Because you're doing something dreadful to her and I've seen it."

"Seen it? Seen what?" The question was suddenly urgent. "What has she shown you?"

Tess looked at him closely. "What's in her face . . . What do you think she's shown me?"

For a moment York did not answer. Tense with the emotion of anticipated murder, he had been caught off guard by what Tess had said. When he had failed to run her down, he had decided to explain it away as a near accident; now he realised he had revealed too much.

"Perhaps she hasn't shown you anything, Miss Davy," he said. "But I'm afraid you now may know too much."

Tess had become aware that the solitariness of the park, so welcome moments before, was suddenly dangerous. Nobody was in sight and what was about to happen would be witnessed only by the now composed cow, staring at her soberly, grass spilling over the edges of its chewing mouth.

"Why did you kill Simon?" she demanded.

"Did I kill Simon?" York smiled mockingly. "Nobody seems to think that I did. Why do you?"

"Because if you didn't kill him, then what the hell is happening? What's wrong with your wife?"

York took a long stride to his left to block her cautious movement towards the fence as she spoke and he saw the spasm of fear that flashed through her eyes.

"That is my business, Miss Davy," he said. "It was very foolish of you to make it yours."

The England number eight flashed his bat high across his faceguard as the bouncer rose up to him, sending it soaring towards the long leg boundary. Millions of television viewers watched anxiously with the crowd as the Australian outfielder sprinted across the grass, calculating the curve of its descent for the critical catch. Augustus Maltravers stared at the screen and saw nothing as he desperately tried to find some flaw in the insanity of something he did not want to be true. As the running fielder held the catch, Maltravers stood up in agitation because the unspeakable would not go away.

"This is *sick*!" All those who knew him as the most easy-going of men would have been startled by the naked, trembling anger in his voice. Downstairs the phone rang and he went to answer it.

"Gus? Peter. I've just heard from Harry Matthews and the police have identified fingerprints on the cricket ball."

"Of course they are," said Maltravers when Peter told him. "I'd already worked that out. Thanks for letting me know."

He went back upstairs and tried to consider the position more calmly. Somehow he had to discover for himself if his repulsive theory was right. He decided to wait until Tess returned; he did not relish doing what had to be done on his own. However uncomfortably, he would just have to wait for her.

Tears of panic ran down Tess's face as she backed away, frantically looking round for help. She was fit enough to run but the tall, athletic York would catch her again in seconds.

"Please, I won't tell anyone!" she begged. "I don't care what's happening between you and Joanna. I'm nothing to do with this place. I'll just go away."

"I'm not stupid, Miss Davy. You know I just tried to kill you. I don't believe you won't tell somebody that."

"I won't! I promise! Please don't . . ." She was standing like a creature petrified by the approach of a snake. As he sprang at her, hands open towards her throat like claws, she screamed.

What happened next happened very swiftly. All York saw was a flash of flying sky and then he was lying on his back squealing with pain, his left arm limp and useless by his side. Tess's face, which had inexplicably vanished just as his hands closed on her neck, reappeared above him. She was panting slightly and pushed back tumbled hair with one hand.

"You have just witnessed one of my lesser ad lib performances as the helpless little woman," she told him crisply, wiping away the remains of created tears. "I imagine you think we're all like that. When I was a student, I had a flat in an area of London where it was not advisable for young women to walk alone at night. I knew those self-defence lessons would come in useful one day."

York groaned and tried to sit up, but she pushed him down again painfully with a foot against his injured shoulder.

"Don't do that," she advised. "It's only dislocated, but I'm quite prepared to break it if necessary. Move slowly and it won't hurt too much. Now I've got to run."

And run she did, taking the shortest route back across the fields, cows scattering as she raced between them, towards the road that led back to Bellringer Street. Tourists stared in surprise as she sprinted past them, out through the arch of the gateway and back to the Penroses. She burst into the kitchen and dashed upstairs to where the television was still on and Maltravers was still not watching it. She leaned against the door frame, gasping with exertion.

"Alister York!" Her chest heaved for air. "He *did* kill Simon!"

"No he didn't," said Maltravers quietly. "Luke Norman did. Peter got it all from Harry Matthews. Luke's fingerprints are all over that ball. They match God knows how many the police have collected in his flat. They'll have taken them from his body as well. I told you that where the ball was found meant that only the case against Luke made sense."

"What?" Tess gulped and flopped in the nearest chair, trying to grasp what Maltravers said and remembering that York had not actually admitted her accusation. "Then why did he just try to kill me?"

"Kill *you*?" Maltravers leapt to his feet and crossed to her. "Are you all right?"

"Yes, of course I am." Tess shook his hand off her shoulder

162

impatiently. "I dislocated his arm with some rusty judo. But if Luke killed Simon, what the hell is happening between Joanna and York?"

Satisfied that she was unharmed, Maltravers looked at her sadly. "That puts it awfully well, I'm afraid. It must be very like hell for her."

"What are you talking about?"

"I warn you, you're not going to like this," he said.

Disbelief, dismay and revulsion invaded Tess as he explained what he had worked out. When he finished she shook her head in violent rejection.

"No! Nobody could do that! God, it's . . ." She shuddered.

"But it fits a lot of unrelated facts together," Maltravers said. "I don't like it either, but we've got to find out if it's true."

"Then let's just tell the police," said Tess.

"Oh, no," said Maltravers. "Not yet at least . . . and possibly never at all. I've had time to think about this. First of all I want to prove it for myself and then . . . I want to see if we can keep it quiet. No questions, there isn't time. How far will York get with that arm?"

"As far as he wants, but not very quickly. He certainly won't be able to drive."

"Right. Then we get to her before he reappears. She's in even worse danger now."

They hurried down Bellringer Street and rang the front door bell of the Yorks' house. As they waited, Maltravers pointed at the still unpainted new putty round the window they had seen the estate workman repairing the morning after the murder.

"But we didn't take any notice at the time, did we?" he remarked as Joanna York opened the door and looked immediately afraid.

"What do you want?" she asked in agitation. "My husband isn't in and . . ."

"We want to come in," said Maltravers.

"What? You can't!" She stepped back, her fear amplifying.

"Please," Maltravers insisted gently. "We want to help you."

"Help me? What do you mean? I don't want . . . Go away."

"Joanna." Tess stopped the girl's protests with the firmness of her voice. "We know."

Maltravers slapped his open hand against the door to stop Joanna York slamming it closed against them. For a moment she pushed helplessly, then the door flew open as she turned and fled into the kitchen and was fumbling with the bolt on the back door as Maltravers ran through and took hold of her.

"Go away!" She struggled in his arms as she pleaded. "Please! He'll hurt me! He'll make me . . ." Her voice was swamped by choking sobs as he turned her round and led her into the small front room and sat her down. Tess knelt in front of her and took hold of both her hands.

"Joanna," she said softly. "He won't hurt you again. He'll never do anything to you again." Her voice stumbled momentarily. "You see, we know what he's been doing to you. That was very cruel of him."

Joanna York looked at her beseechingly.

"You know about . . . ?" The brittle voice faded in disbelief as Tess nodded. "But how can you? I never told . . . I couldn't . . . I . . ." She stopped as emotion tore through her and when her voice returned it was very faint. "I'm so ashamed . . . ashamed . . . please leave me alone."

"I'm going upstairs," Maltravers said to Tess. "That's where it will be."

In such a small house, it took him only moments to find the main bedroom and he went to the wardrobe in the corner, pausing a long moment before the impassive door, certain now beyond all disbelief that he was right. He stiffened himself, then took hold of the handle and pulled the door open.

Inside was the skeleton of Tom Bostock, Dunford's Vincent's tie grotesquely knotted beneath the scoffing skull. Pushing down his revulsion, Maltravers leaned forward and peered at the grey, scabrous teeth and saw a slight smear of pink on two of them.

164

"Sweet Jesus," he murmured as tears of pity pricked his eyes. He was the third person to see that corruption and, at whatever risk to himself, he wanted to be the last.

The problem was, how could that be accomplished? He closed the wardrobe door again, frantically going over a scheme, certainly illegal but just possibly feasible, when he heard a key in the front door below him. He dashed down and reached the bottom of the stairs in the corner of the room as Alister York stepped awkwardly into the house. Tess leapt to her feet and stood protectively in front of Joanna, eyes blazing.

"You are the most evil man I have ever met in my life." Her voice was quiet with icy fury. "You are disgusting! They taught me how to kill people on that course and if you go anywhere near this girl, that's exactly what I'm going to do."

"Tess," Maltravers said warningly and her face was bitter as she turned to him. "Just take Joanna up the hill. I'll handle this."

Tess softened again as she put her arm round Joanna's shoulders and helped her to her feet. Then she led her out of the house, placing herself between the woman and her husband. York looked at them both contemptuously, then stepped aside to let them pass, closing the door behind them with his good arm.

"I expect you've called the police," he said to Maltravers.

"No." Maltravers stepped off the final stair. "I want to talk to you."

"Well there's nothing I wish to discuss with you."

"Oh I think there is," said Maltravers. "Just think for a moment. We could have rung the police as soon as Tess got back from the park and laid a charge of attempted murder against you. Hasn't it occurred to you to wonder why we came here instead?"

York regarded him suspiciously. Finding Maltravers and Tess in his own house – where he had painfully made his way because there was nowhere else to go – had surprised him. After getting away with so much, he knew he had made a critical mistake. He had assumed he would find the police waiting for him, not Maltravers and the woman he had tried to kill. He sensed that something was being offered to him.

"Then why did you?" he asked guardedly.

"Just sit down for a minute," said Maltravers. "I still don't believe what I now know and I'd like to check my thoughts with you. Then we might have something to talk about."

Weary with pain, York took a chair next to the door and Maltravers went across the room and looked upwards through the window at the first storey of the Darbys' house on the other side of the street.

"When you found Simon's body over there – incidentally, I know you didn't kill him, even though I'm positive you meant to – you took his tie off. You then wrapped it round the other cricket ball that was still on the desk and threw it straight across the road through this window. Simple enough for a cricketer of your ability. Later you had one of the estate workers repair the window and said it had been broken by vandals. Right?" York made no reply.

"That explains the odd loose ends about the murder," Maltravers continued. "Luke Norman had taken the ball he used to kill Simon with him and threw it away in the park – the police have it now but that's irrelevant. The question is, why would you do such a thing? And I worked that out this afternoon from something I remembered saying to Tess about the butler in the Pembury chapel. The skeleton in the cupboard."

"While you're getting to the point, I'd like a drink," York interrupted. "It's in the cabinet over there. Whisky straight for me and you may as well help yourself."

Maltravers poured the drinks, disinterested in the intellectual satisfaction of unravelling something so awful. He still had his back to York when he spoke again.

"Not many people know the weird story of the woman who

had a son in India, do they?" He turned to York with the glasses in his hand and passed him the whisky. "It's very fragmentary, but basically she received a letter from him asking her to find someone to make him six shirts for some unknown reason. He added that whoever did it must be someone without any cares in the world. The mother was understandably mystified, but did as he asked and eventually found a woman who seemed perfect. But when she went to see her, the woman took her upstairs and showed her a human skeleton in a cupboard. It was her former lover . . . and her husband made her kiss it every night."

Maltravers glanced upwards as he continued. "The mother wrote back to her son with this news and he replied that he had been convinced that everyone in the world had their troubles – his that he was to be hanged. His letter ended, 'Mother, mother, there is a skeleton in every cupboard!'"

Maltravers took a sip of his gin and looked at York with something like sympathy.

"I can't remember meeting anybody else before who knows the story behind the old saying. And, dear God, you must be the only person who would act it out again."

York looked away from him.

"And I've just thought of something else," Maltravers went on. "Let me think it through . . . You were out to an untypically bad stroke in the cricket match weren't you? You knew Dunford would stay at the wicket . . . giving you time to go back to the house to steal his tie or something like it prior to killing him. You wanted to really ram it home to your wife who that skeleton represented. That little girl said she had seen a ghost in the family quarters, and to small children a ghost is something white . . . like a man in cricket flannels. Am I right there as well? Oh, forget it, it doesn't matter. Nobody in their right minds would believe a word of it anyway. Stealing Tom Bostock's skeleton was no problem for someone like you who worked in the house. But you had to do it quickly because of the plans to bury him."

"When you said you wanted to talk, I didn't realise you just wanted to demonstrate your cleverness," York said sarcastically. "I can't see why I should be subjected to your self-satisfaction but, if it pleases your conceit, you're quite correct. Now you'll be able to impress everyone with your remarkable intelligence, won't you?"

"No," said Maltravers. "I just wanted to make sure I'd got it right – conceit if you wish – but I don't want to tell anybody else about this. I want to offer you something instead."

"There's nothing I want from you," York replied curtly.

"What about freedom? And avoiding the contempt people will have for you if it all comes out? Doesn't that matter?"

"Does it matter to you?"

"In your case, no," Maltravers told him bluntly. "In your wife's case, a great deal. Listen. Your attempt to murder Tess will not be reported to the police if you agree to leave Joanna and never – and I mean never – see her again. You've had your vengeance, now let her go. That's between you and your conscience, but wouldn't you prefer that your family and friends never knew about it?"

Maltravers noticed York's eyes flash past him at something in the other corner of the room. He turned and looked but could see nothing that seemed significant. On the wall was a framed photograph of York's father who he knew would eradicate his son from his life if he ever learned what had happened. Correct, strong and mercilessly unforgiving, he would accept as normal that his son had dominated his wife; that he had broken the law and brought disgrace upon himself would be contemptible. Irreparably scarred by his father's treatment and conditioning of him, York could not bear the thought that having grown to admire him – even perversely to love him – he might lose him.

"What about . . . ?" He gestured with his glass towards the upstairs of the house.

"That's my part of the deal," said Maltravers. "Leave it with me. I'll be very careful. I don't want the police asking me difficult questions."

York was silent again, absorbing all that Maltravers had said, recognising the escape route it offered him.

"Don't expect any thanks," he said finally. "I find your sort pitiful. You're weak, filled with ludicrous kindness. Too many people think that kindness is important. It's not. I will accept your offer, but don't delude yourself that my conscience will trouble me. What I did was right, although you will never be able to understand that."

"Let's face it, you and I may as well be from different planets," said Maltravers. "You find me pitiful, I think you're an obscenity. But sod all that. I'm doing this for your wife. If I could find a way of protecting her and dragging you through hell at the same time, I'd happily take it. Let's just hope for both our sakes that you and I never have anything to do with each other again."

The two men stared at each other for a moment, then both turned away, each with disgust, but one with a certain sorrow.

Chapter Twelve

Alone in the house, Maltravers contemplated the bizarre, incredible and potentially disastrous situation in which he had placed himself. A few minutes earlier York had left for the hospital in a taxi to have his arm attended to, Tess and Joanna were at the Penroses, Maltravers was left to deal with the remains of a dead highwayman, twice abused for human hatred. He could conjure up in his mind the strange image of the fourth Earl of Pembury keeping his secret appointment year by year, candle-cast shadows on the cellar wall as he raised his glass in a cruel and mocking toast; history gave that some sort of grotesque perspective. What he could not conceive was the picture of what had been happening in the past couple of days, a young, pretty and vulnerable woman pressing her lips against a skull's rictus smile, warm and living flesh on dead bone.

He shuddered and went back upstairs, forcing control into himself like someone steeling their stomach to clear up vomit. The sight of Dunford's tie again made him retch momentarily, then he carefully removed it and placed it in his pocket. In the bathroom airing cupboard he found a sheet and spread it out on the bedroom floor, then, using his handkerchief to avoid leaving fingerprints, he lifted the skeleton off the hook from which it was suspended and laid it in the centre of the sheet, pulling the corners together to form a rough sack.

He peered cautiously out of the front door before leaving the house. Two women were standing talking towards the bottom of Bellringer Street, but otherwise there was nobody in sight. As he walked swiftly up the hill, the constant clicking from the bundle he was carrying sounded frighteningly distinct and he could only hope that anyone who saw him from a distance would assume he was carrying a bag of washing back from the launderette in the square; certainly no one would imagine the truth.

"Is that you Gus?" Tess's voice from the dining room as he entered the house sounded relieved. "We're in here."

"Just a minute," he called back then went upstairs and pushed the clattering bones of Tom Bostock under their bed. When he went down again, Joanna York was looking more composed, although the dried tears which had smeared her make-up across her face made her look like a melting and helpless wax doll. He sat down next to her and took hold of her hand encouragingly.

"It's all right," he said firmly. "I've talked to him and he's agreed to certain things . . . No, just listen to me."

Small frowns flickered across her face like a bewildered child listening to the explanation of something very difficult as Maltravers told her the agreement he had made with York.

"But that's not right," she protested when he had finished. "Tess has told me that he tried to kill her and . . . what he did to me. You're letting him get away with it. You mustn't."

"Yes we must," Maltravers contradicted. "Joanna, if all this comes out and Alister is punished, what will happen to you? Every newspaper in the country will run this story, everybody will pity you, but a lot will despise you. Isn't it worth him getting away with it to stop that happening?"

Joanna looked at him like someone drowning staring at a lifeline thrown from nowhere. "But how can . . . ? It would mean . . . You can't do it, it's too dangerous for you."

"Not that dangerous." Maltravers leaned forward, reinforcing what he was saying. "And we will make you a promise. Tess and I will *never* tell anyone what has happened."

They both watched her carefully through a very long silence. Battered with torment, unbalanced by the relief of rescue, she was shakily trying to find some stability. When she spoke again, her voice was soft and deliberate as she appeared slowly to accept.

"I hear what you're saying to me and I think I understand it. I'm sorry, but I can't cope with it all at the moment." She breathed in very deeply and straightened up in the chair. "I'll try. I owe you both that."

"Good girl," said Maltravers. "First of all, is there anywhere you can go?"

"My parents." Joanna York spoke with growing reassurance. "They never liked Alister and will accept that I've left him."

"Where do they live?" Maltravers asked.

"Ramshill . . . it's about twenty miles away, but I don't drive."

"We'll take you," said Maltravers. "You'll need some things but you're not going back into that house, even while your husband is away at the hospital. Tell Tess where to find them and she'll – " He suddenly stopped and looked guilty. "Christ, I closed the door behind me! And you've not got your handbag. How do we get back in?"

Joanna York reached up to the neckline of her dress and pulled out a slender chain with a key dangling from it.

"Mummy made me do this when I was little," she said. "I still do it in case I forget."

She spoke as if the habit was perfectly normal, but Maltravers and Tess were shaken to see the little girl who lived in the woman's body, the child who had cried in the terror of the night.

"My make-up's upstairs," Tess said, standing up. "You can fix your face while I collect what you want."

The offer caught Maltravers unawares and he was unable to stop Tess taking Joanna to the room where he had hidden the skeleton, but reassured himself that it would not be visible. She had never asked about it and was probably trying to remove it from her memory. He heard Tess leave the house and when she returned about twenty minutes later he was still in the front room looking out at the church.

"You do realise what we've got ourselves into, don't you?" she asked, putting Joanna's case down by the door.

"Just about." He turned and faced her. "But I imagine we'll survive and I'm bloody sure Joanna won't if it all comes out. We're the only chance she's got . . . so that's all right, isn't it Best Beloved?"

"Oh, yes, it's just so furiously insane that I'm still coming to terms with it. What did you do with that damned skeleton?"

"Well, purely as a temporary measure . . ." Maltravers stopped as Joanna came back, the ravages across her face at least cosmetically masked. He smiled at her. "You look better already. Let's get you home."

Joanna remained silent in the back of the car during the journey and neither Tess nor Maltravers could think of anything to say. They drew up outside the house and Tess turned round in her seat as Maltravers went to take the suitcase out of the boot. She handed the girl a piece of paper.

"My address and phone number," she said. "Call me whenever you want, particularly when the blue meanies strike. God made shoulders for crying on."

"I've been thinking," said Joanna, taking the paper and folding it in her hands. "I can understand why he wanted to kill Simon, he thought there had been something between us. He was wrong, but he's so possessive he really would have done it. Thank you for assuring me he didn't, that helps. I don't know what to think about the last couple of nights except that he must be mad in some way. He had a very strange childhood and has some funny ideas. What I can't forgive him for is that he tried to kill you when all you had tried to do was help me. That was dreadful."

"Forget it, because it doesn't matter," Tess told her. "I'm not bone china and I looked after myself. What matters is you picking up the pieces again. Don't let him win."

Tess paused, uncertain about raising something she could not understand and wanted to know.

"Why did you marry him?" she asked gently.

Joanna looked surprised. "Why? Because I loved him. I

173

loved him very much indeed. Why else should I have married him?"

"Sorry," Tess said apologetically. "Stupid question."

Joanna got out of the car and Maltravers handed her the case.

"I can't think of anything to say to you," she said. "I'm too confused. But I know you're taking an enormous risk to help me. I'm just so scared that I might let you down."

"I don't think you will," he told her. "After all, you never let Alister down and he didn't deserve that. I hope you think we do."

As he watched the slender figure walk away from him up the garden path, he felt it had been a thought worth planting. The problems he would have with the police if she cracked and blurted it all out to her parents were irrelevant; the danger to her self-respect, perhaps even her sanity mattered much more. He climbed back into the car and they drove away without speaking. After a few minutes, Maltravers turned on the radio.

" . . . Emburey seven not out. England won by one wicket. After the match, the England captain Mike Gatting spoke to . . ."

Maltravers leaned forward and switched the set off. "Funny, that seemed important earlier this afternoon. Strange how life goes on in the middle of everyone's crises."

The normality of finding Peter and the children at home when they returned was almost unnatural. Full of questions about her new baby brother, Emma showed Tess a picture she had painted at school, a vaguely female shape labelled "Mummy" with a tiny stick figure coming out of its distended stomach.

"And that's the baby," she explained excitedly. "And that's his cot and that's his teddy and this is his hot water bottle and this is . . ."

Tess smiled and nodded helplessly.

"What have you been doing with yourselves then?" Peter asked as he handed Maltravers a can of beer from the fridge.

"Nothing special. Tess went for a walk while I watched the cricket for a bit then we went for a drive." As he ripped open the seal and poured the drink into a glass, Maltravers reflected that, apart from a few salient details, it was a perfectly accurate summary. He took a much-needed swallow. "Anyway, at least it looks as though Simon's murder has been cleared up."

"Harry says the police appear satisfied," Peter confirmed. "They had Luke's prints from his flat and they're very clear on the ball. I must say you didn't seem surprised when I told you."

"It was obvious, nothing else made sense." Maltravers took another mouthful before adding a question of his own. "What are they doing about the other ball and the tie?"

"According to Harry, they're not too bothered. They reckon anyone could have nicked the ball during the party and is too scared to admit it and the tie is just an odd loose end. They'll keep the file open in case anything happens, but that's about it."

"They're probably right," said Maltravers. "I can't see any way in which those other items matter."

Somehow the evening passed. They entertained the children and sent them off to bed before Peter returned with a Chinese takeaway after visiting Susan. They listened to him talking about his second son, his wife and his marriage without betraying the moments of abstraction when the events of the afternoon flooded back into their minds. Local gossip would swiftly inform Bellringer Street that Joanna York had left her husband, but the collapse of a marriage which most people had thought strange would not surprise anyone or hold their interest for long. York had every reason to keep quiet and Maltravers would have been interested if he had known that while they were talking the secretary was typing out his letter of resignation to Lord Pembury, wincing in discomfort and rekindled frustration as movement sent shots of pain down the arm in a sling.

When they went to their room, Tess flopped in full-length exhaustion on the bed.

"Do you remember how drained I was after playing Brecht at Chichester? It was a breeze compared to this. Thank God we're leaving in the morning."

"Yes, but there is still the little matter of Tom Bostock to deal with," Maltravers reminded her. She sat up, abruptly re-animated.

"Shit! I thought you sorted that out. Where is he?"

"Under the bed."

"Under the bed," Tess repeated tonelessly. "The bed on which I am now sitting. Of course he is. Where else would he be? What shall we do with him? I know, let's take him home with us. A little souvenir of the holiday. Marvellous conversation piece at dinner parties. 'Oh, it's just a little thing we picked up in Old Capley. Amazingly cheap. It only cost us our sanity and a man's . . .'" The nonsense and deliberate rising tone of artificial hysteria in her voice were not enough to hold off the swarming emotions of the sudden return to the knowledge of all they had been through. The protective layer of acting fell away and was replaced by a look of anguish.

"Oh Christ, stop me joking about it, Gus! Simon's dead and Joanna's nearly been destroyed and I'm the big supergirl who can look after herself and . . ." She started to cry.

Maltravers crossed the room and sat with his arms around her as the tears washed out everything that had been building up inside. After a few minutes he felt her pull herself together and relax as she sat up again and leaned back against the headboard of the bed.

"I'm all right now," she told him. "So what are you going to do about . . .?" Her eyes glanced downwards.

"I'm taking him home. It should be safe enough in about a couple of hours. I've worked it all out."

"Before you tell me, just take him from underneath the bed," Tess interrupted. "I'm too tired to get off and I don't want him that close to me."

Maltravers knelt on the floor and carefully pulled out the

sheet and its contents. Tess shuddered as a corner fell away, revealing a glimpse of the skull, and turned away in agitation.

"Cover him up. He's too horrible."

Maltravers lifted the sheet and placed it by the bedroom door, as far out of Tess's line of vision as he could manage. Then he told her what he meant to do.

"Do you think it will work?" she asked.

"I think there's a reasonable chance. As far as we know, the theft has never been reported and there's been enough drama at Edenbridge House in the past couple of days. I think they'll want to avoid any more. With a bit of luck, they'll just take him back in, keep quiet about it and eventually bury him as Lady Pembury wants. Even if they do call in the police, they're very unlikely to connect it with the murder – or with me."

"What about Alister York? He'll realise what you've done."

"Of course he will, but he'll want to keep it quiet more than anybody else."

Tess looked at her watch; it was nearly midnight. "What a weird vigil. It's crazy of course, but so is everything else about this."

At first they tried to read, but it was no use; concentration on the words was constantly vandalised by the silent presence in the corner of the room. Finally, they just sat side by side, each wrapped in their own thoughts as the night crept away. When the church clock struck its single note for half-past one, Maltravers could stand it no longer.

"It's as safe now as any time," he said.

"How long do you think it will take?"

"No more than half an hour I hope."

"Do you want me to come with you?"

"No, I can manage on my own. If I'm not back by half-past two, start praying."

He rolled off the bed and crept quietly across the bedroom floor, picked up the sheet very carefully then tiptoed out of the room and downstairs. Tess sat still for a few minutes, then

177

reached down and found her handbag from which she took her manicure set and occupied herself in unnecessarily attending to her nails.

Above St Barbara's a racing moon swam between silvered flotsam of cloud and the trees in the churchyard whirred softly in the crisp whisper of the night breeze. A shadow among shadows, Maltravers made his way through the gravestones, carrying death between the dead in its strange winding sheet. He passed beneath the dark mass of the building and round to where a low wall formed the boundary with Edenbridge Park. He was just able to reach over and place his burden with a faint rattle on the ground the other side before cautiously scrambling after it. A hundred yards in front of him was a small copse of trees with the outline of the house, about a quarter of a mile away, just visible beyond them. As he hesitated before crossing the first open space, a fox coughed in the distance; the trees were full of tiny nocturnal noises as he crept among them. Emerging into the open again, an owl, swift and soundless, swooped out of the gloom and brushed the top of his head. There was a clatter of bones as he ducked in panic and for a few moments he crouched there, heart almost erupting and momentarily faint.

"This is ridiculous," he muttered as his breath gasped back, then he remembered Joanna York's face and moved on towards the turrets of the house, slates gleaming like blue ice in spasmodic moonlight. He had forgotten the gravel approaches and the crunch of every step sounded to him like a shriek in the silence; he kept stopping, convinced he had heard a sound which would mean discovery and almost comically dropping Tom Bostock with a splintering crash as he fled. But there were no sudden shouts of outrage, no terrifying appearance of approaching lights as he stepped off the gravel and climbed the wide semi-circle of steps, keeping close to the wall.

Finally he reached the front door where he and Tess had last stood when Simon had said goodnight to them after the concert – and had then gone to tell Lord Pembury about the disappearance of the skeleton. Delicately, Maltravers laid the sheet down on the flagstones and opened it out; the bony remains of the wandering highwayman shone with a faint phosphorescence in the cold white light. Using his handkerchief again, he placed his hand against the top of the skull and inched the skeleton out. The empty eye sockets stared up at the infinite spaces of the sky. Maltravers was about to go when he remembered something. Kneeling down again, he moistened a corner of the handkerchief with his tongue and carefully wiped away the traces of Joanna's lipstick from the front teeth; then he stood up and looked for the last time at the mortal remains of the man whose adventures in death had been so rare and hideous.

"*Requiescat in pace*," he murmured. "Both you and Simon."

Then he folded the sheet and stole away, leaving Tom Bostock awaiting admittance at the door of his ancestors.

Five hours later, a maid opened the front door of Edenbridge House and her scream streaked like an arrow across the morning peace of the park before she fainted. Lord Pembury was summoned and gave immediate instructions that Tom Bostock should be replaced in his coffin and the cellar door locked. It had all been a tasteless prank, he decided, and gave strict orders that his staff were to say nothing whatever about it. Once the burial of his son was over, the matter would be dealt with as arranged.

Tom Bostock was to make one last journey to Bellringer Street, carrying with him a secret unguessed and unguessable.

"You're looking tired." Peter looked at Maltravers carefully as they shook hands. "Are you all right?"

"I'm fine. I just didn't sleep very well for some reason."

"I thought I heard you moving about in the night. Sure there's nothing you want? Paracetamol or something?"

"I'm OK, don't worry. Probably just a bit of reaction. It's been a funny few days one way and another."

Peter looked apologetic. "Come again. Susan will be sorry to have missed you and . . . you know." His look covered words he could not find.

"I know," Maltravers assured him. "Give her our love and take care of yourselves."

The children were suddenly all about, excitedly saying goodbye with Emma holding out some soft toy that had to be kissed, then there was a waving of retreating hands as Maltravers and Tess drove away. He stopped at the T-junction at the bottom of Bellringer Street to let another car pass.

"Did you notice that old framed map on Peter and Susan's staircase?" he asked. "It shows where all the pubs were in Bellringer Street in the old days. The Yorks' house used to be the Maid's Head, which is where Tom Bostock was arrested with his mistress. Strange to think that he may have been kissed in that room before."

Tess made no reply but stared out of the window as Maltravers drove on, catching a glimpse of the shop where they had first seen Joanna York crack up. She found the inevitable sign above the window ironically painful. It said "Family Butcher".

Chapter Thirteen

Varnished with rain, gold, fire-red and cinnamon leaves flecked the grey gravestones of St Barbara's churchyard or lay in piles like dank rag rugs under their parent trees and along the edges of pathways shining with a damp film. Their autumn livery and the faded green of the grass seemed to hold the only colours in a monochrome world as a fine spray oozed down on to the leaden church out of seamless charcoal clouds. The quietness was only broken by the muffled tolling of a single bell, the dull repeated notes striding relentlessly from the flint tower of the church and vibrating down the canyon of Bell-ringer Street like the retreating drum of an army of the dead. In the gloom of the late October afternoon, the mourners shuffling behind the coffin of Tom Bostock were figures cut from black paper, moving slowly through the seeping curtain of drizzle. Lord and Lady Pembury led them, followed by Oliver Hawkhurst and his wife, the new Edenbridge House secretary and a handful of estate workers. Drawn out of macabre curiosity, a small group stood by the main gate watching the strange procession for the very private funeral pass up the path to where the vicar of Capley – another sable figure – waited in the porch. As the coffin reached him, he bowed solemnly then turned and led them all into the building, his fading voice intoning the Christian incantation for a human soul of whom all will be forgiven.

"I am the resurrection and the life, saith the Lord: he that believeth in me, though he were dead, yet shall he live: and whosoever liveth and believeth in me shall never die . . ."

The doors closed and only the wet, whispering sounds of the smearing rain remained. Standing alone to one side by the door of the vestry beneath a black umbrella, Augustus Maltravers was immobile with recollection of poisonous events. After a few moments' contemplation that so much had finally reached its end, he brought himself back to normality and walked towards where the little crowd of the curious was dispersing. As he neared the gates, he saw Joanna York looking impassively at the church. She smiled slightly as he walked up to her.

"I didn't expect to see you here," he said.

"I wasn't going to come at first, but then I thought it might lay some ghosts."

"And has it?"

"I don't know." Slender shoulders shrugged slightly under her olive-green tweed coat. "Perhaps. I'll have to see."

Her saddened eyes went back to the church for some final contemplation then she appeared to pull herself together again.

"Thank Tess for her letter," she said. "I'll reply before I leave in a couple of weeks."

"Where are you going?"

"New Zealand. My sister lives in Wellington. She always was the strong one. She'll look after me. It's . . . about as far as I can go."

"And Alister?" Maltravers ventured cautiously.

"That's just between the solicitors now. He's agreed to a divorce after two years' separation and I don't think he'll go back on that." She looked up at him. "I don't expect I'll see you again. It sounds inadequate, but thank you for everything you both did. I won't let you down. Give my love to Tess."

There was nothing else to say as they faced each other, two people in the rain at the top of Bellringer Street in the dying light of the dripping melancholy day.

"Goodbye," Maltravers said gently and leaned down towards her. She pulled away abruptly.

"No . . . I'm sorry. I don't like being kissed any more."

The flash of sadness and pain in her face caught him before she turned and walked rapidly down the hill. He watched until she vanished from sight round the corner opposite the square, then crossed the road and rang the Penroses' bell. Susan opened the door, smiling with her infant son in her arms.

"What a day for a funeral," she said. "Come on in."

Maltravers lowered his umbrella and shook it on the step before entering.

"You look awfully sad." Susan looked at him closely. "What on earth are you so upset about Tom Bostock for?"

"I just found it rather moving." Maltravers took off his coat and hung it on the pillar at the foot of the bannisters. "Here, give him to me and I promise not to drop him."

Susan passed the baby over and Maltravers looked at him seriously.

"'In everyone there sleeps a sense of life lived according to love. To some it means the difference they could make by loving others, but across most it sweeps as all they might have done had they been loved.' A very perceptive man called Philip Larkin wrote that."

The baby squinted at him, then pushed a tiny hand clumsily against his face, unable to comprehend the gibberish that grown-ups talked.